MORE PRAISE FOR BABYMOUSE!

"Sassy, smart . . .
Babymouse is here
to stay."
—The Horn Book Magazine

"Young readers
will happily
fall in line."
—Kirkus Reviews

"The brother-sister creative team hits the mark
with humor, sweetness, and characters so genuine
they can pass for real kids." —Booklist

"Babymouse is spunky, ambitious,
and, at times, a total dweeb."
—School Library Journal

Be sure to read **all** the **BABYMOUSE** books:

- #1 BABYMOUSE: Queen of the World!
- #2 BABYMOUSE: Our Hero
- #3 BABYMOUSE: Beach Babe
- #4 BABYMOUSE: Rock Star
- #5 BABYMOUSE: Heartbreaker
- #6 CAMP BABYMOUSE
- #7 BABYMOUSE: Skater Girl
- #8 BABYMOUSE: Puppy Love
- #9 BABYMOUSE: Monster Mash
- #10 BABYMOUSE: The Musical

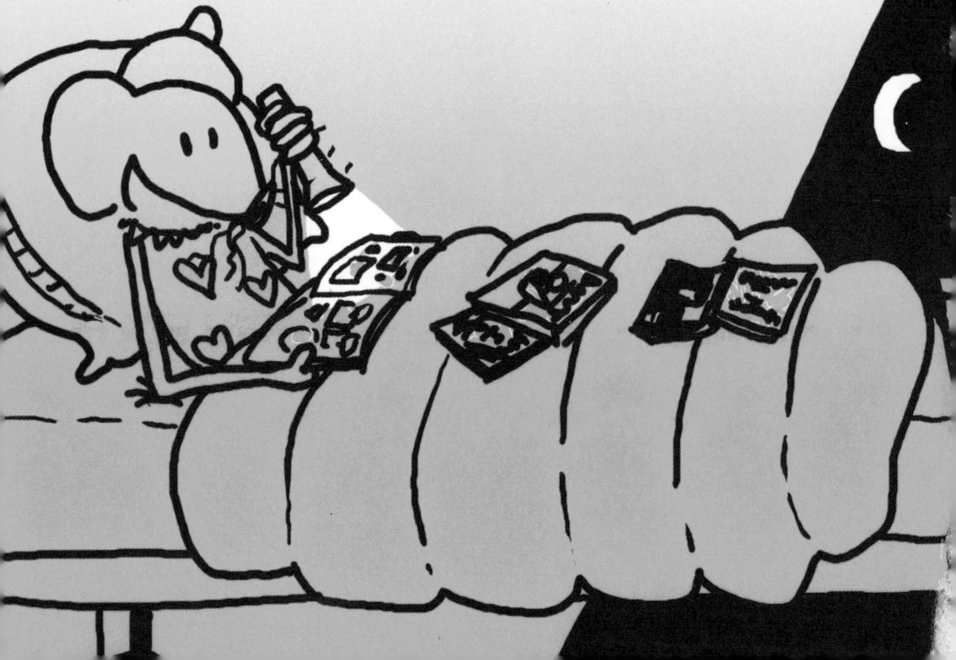

CAMP BABYMOUSE

BY JENNIFER L. HOLM & MATTHEW HOLM

RANDOM HOUSE 🏠 NEW YORK

HEY! I'M **NOT** A WORK OF FICTION!

Copyright © 2007 by Jennifer Holm and Matthew Holm. All rights reserved. Published in the United States by Random House Children's Books, a division of Random House, Inc., New York.

www.randomhouse.com/kids
www.babymouse.com

Educators and librarians, for a variety of teaching tools, visit us at
www.randomhouse.com/teachers

Library of Congress Cataloging-in-Publication Data
Holm, Jennifer L.
Babymouse : Camp Babymouse / Jennifer L. Holm and Matthew Holm.
    p.   cm.
ISBN: 978-0-375-83988-7 (trade) — ISBN: 978-0-375-93988-4 (lib. bdg.)
I. Graphic novels. I. Holm, Matthew. II. Title. III. Title: Camp Babymouse.
PN6727.H592B26 2007   741.5—dc22   2006050391

MANUFACTURED IN MALAYSIA   10

RANDOM HOUSE and colophon are registered trademarks of Random House, Inc.

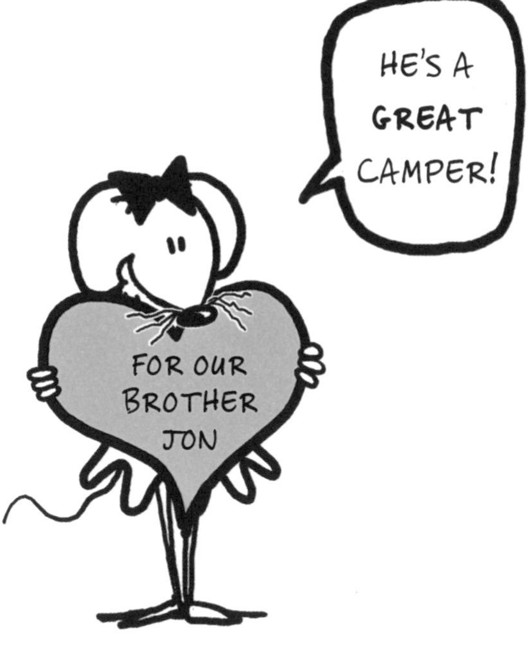
FOR OUR BROTHER JON
HE'S A **GREAT** CAMPER!

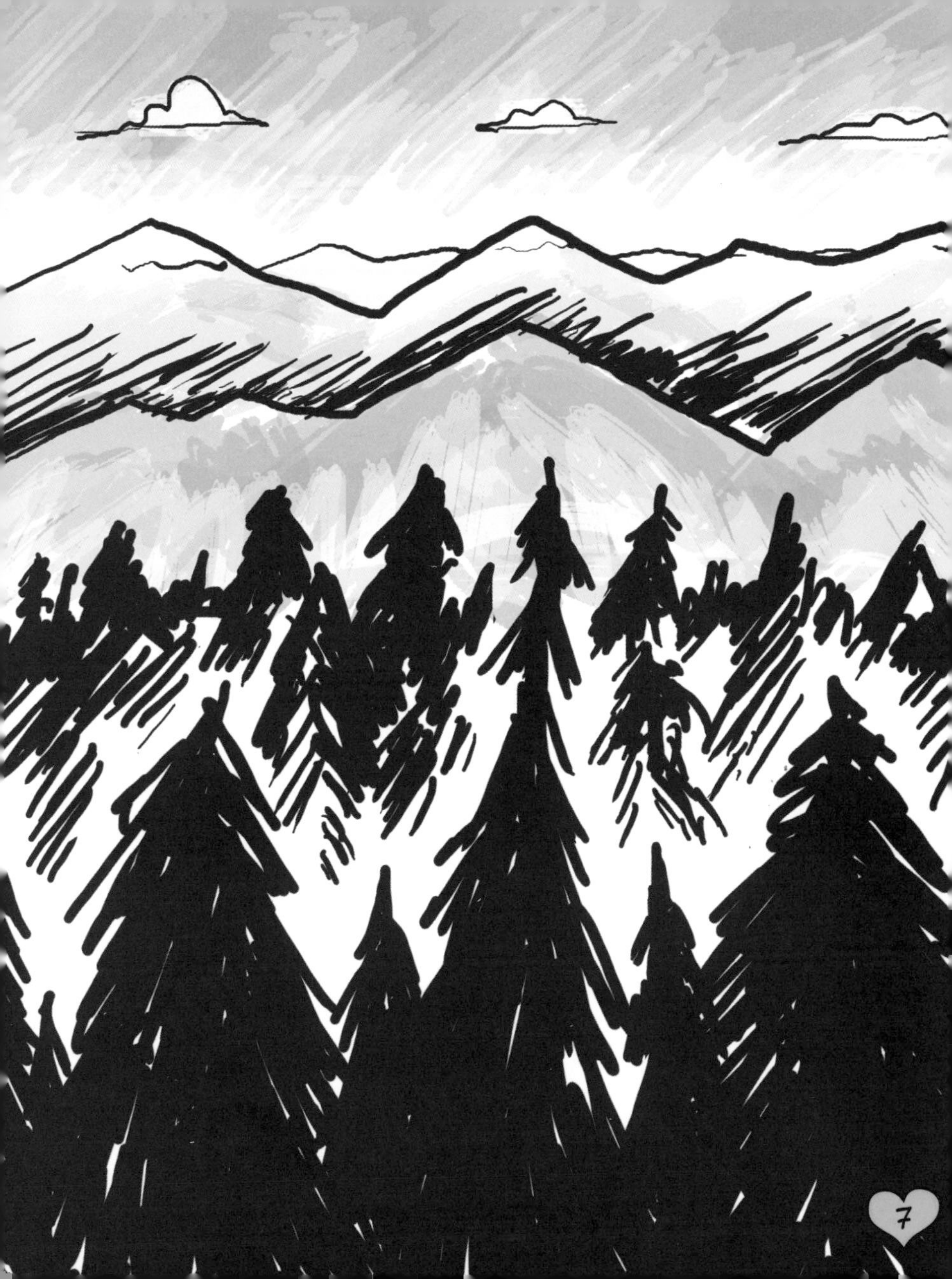

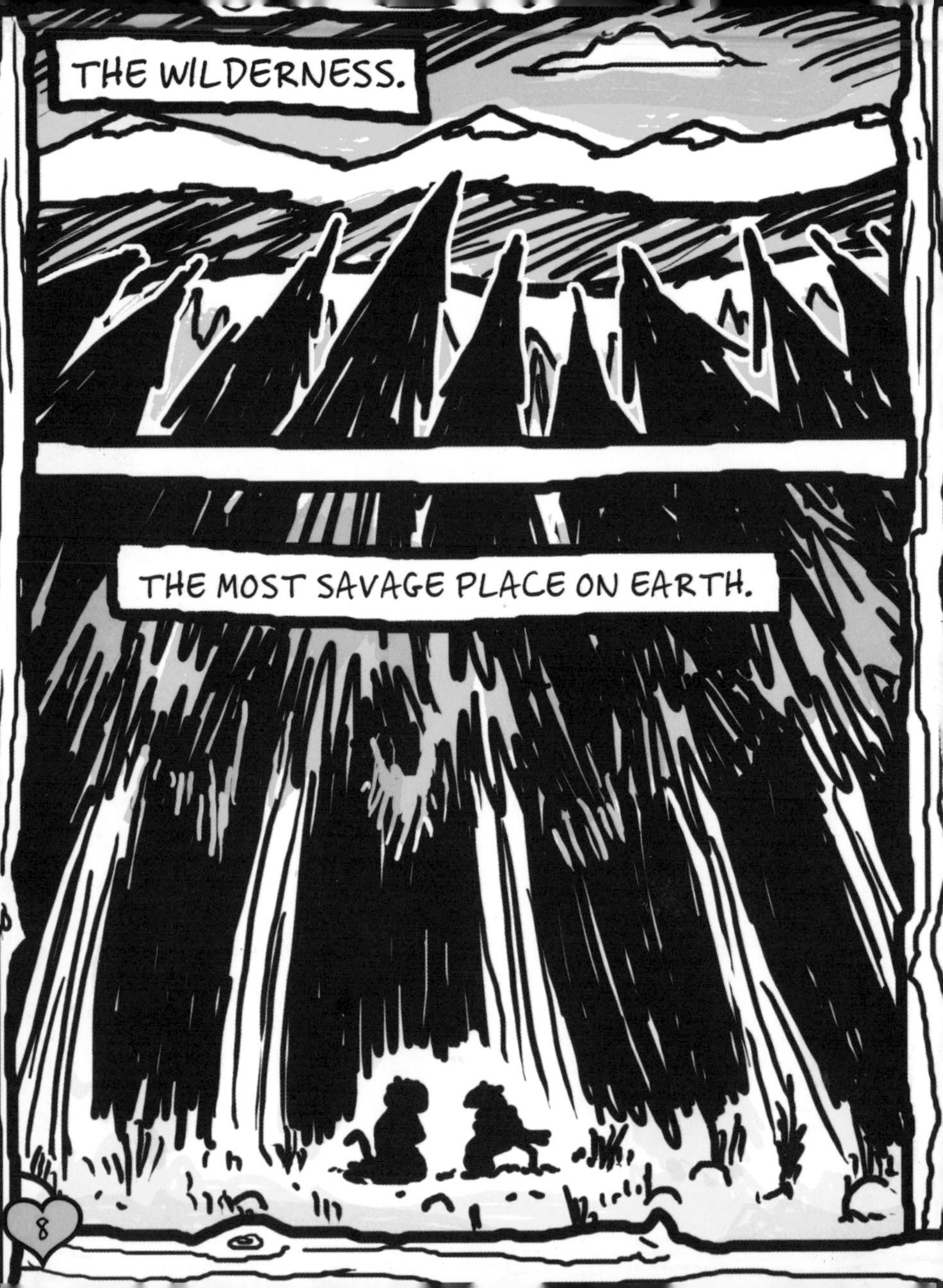
THE WILDERNESS.
THE MOST SAVAGE PLACE ON EARTH.

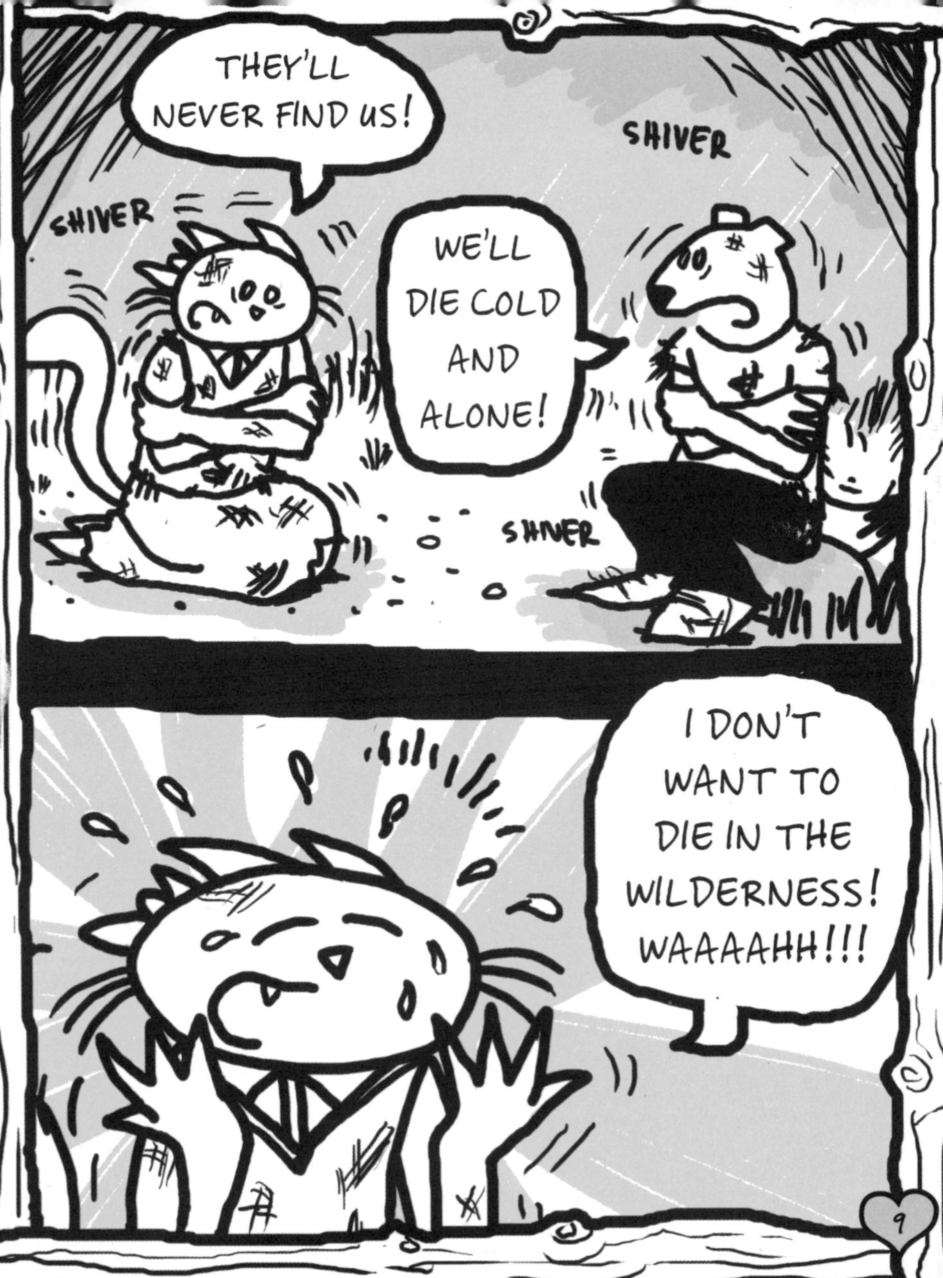
THEY'LL NEVER FIND US!
SHIVER
SHIVER
WE'LL DIE COLD AND ALONE!
SHIVER
I DON'T WANT TO DIE IN THE WILDERNESS! WAAAAHH!!!

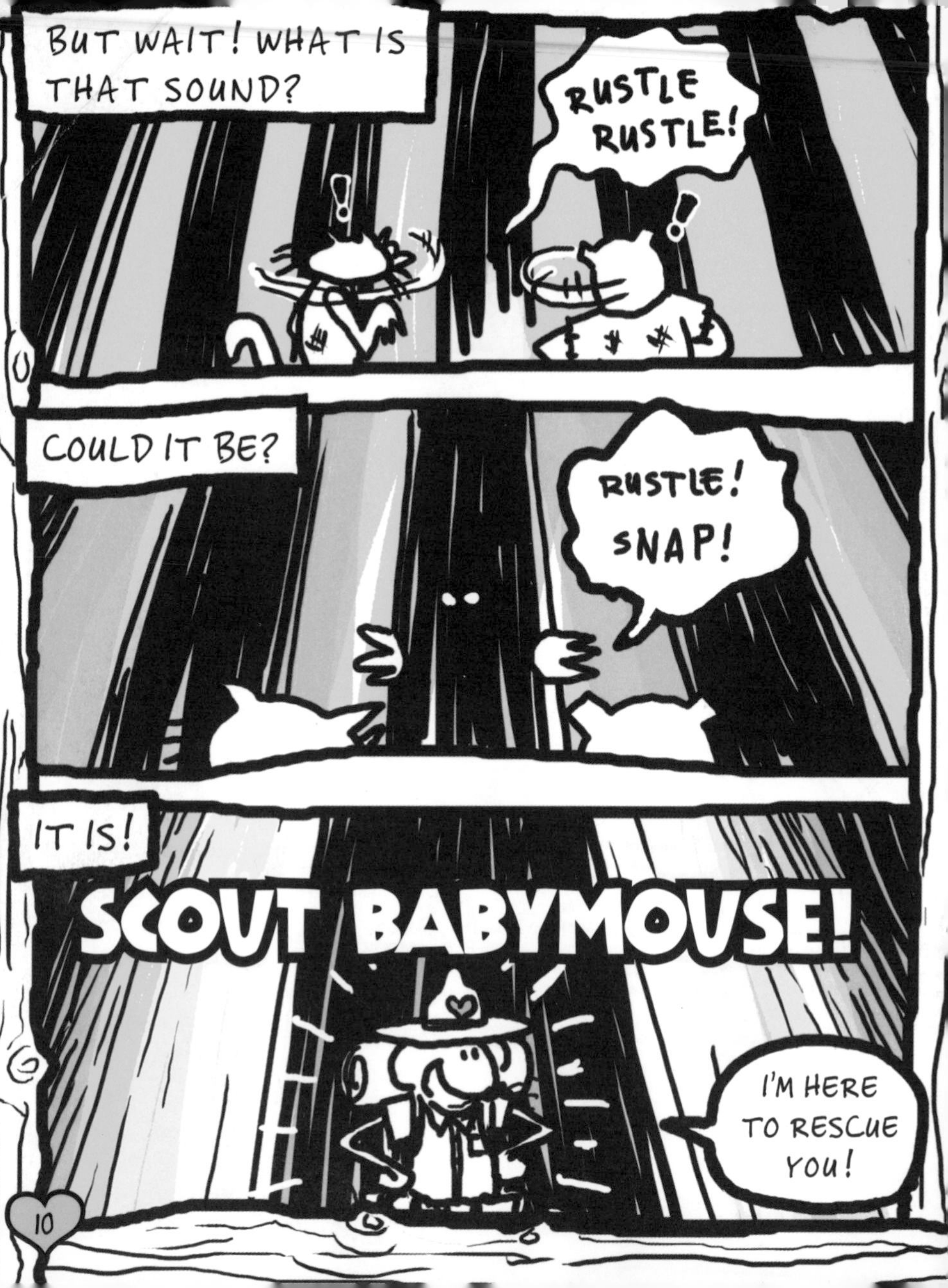
BUT WAIT! WHAT IS THAT SOUND?
RUSTLE RUSTLE!
!
!
COULD IT BE?
RUSTLE! SNAP!
IT IS!
SCOUT BABYMOUSE!
I'M HERE TO RESCUE YOU!

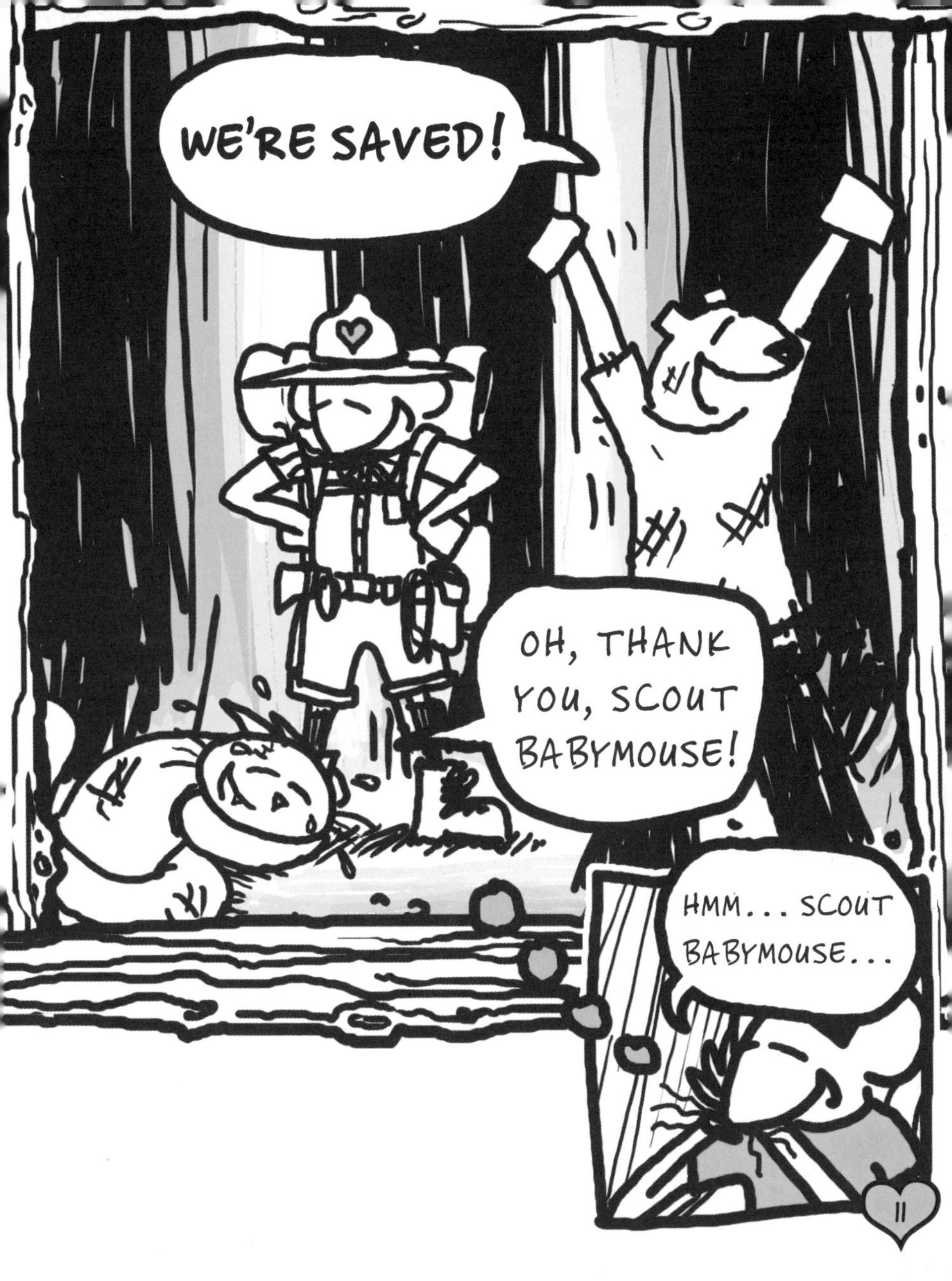
WE'RE SAVED!
OH, THANK YOU, SCOUT BABYMOUSE!
HMM... SCOUT BABYMOUSE...

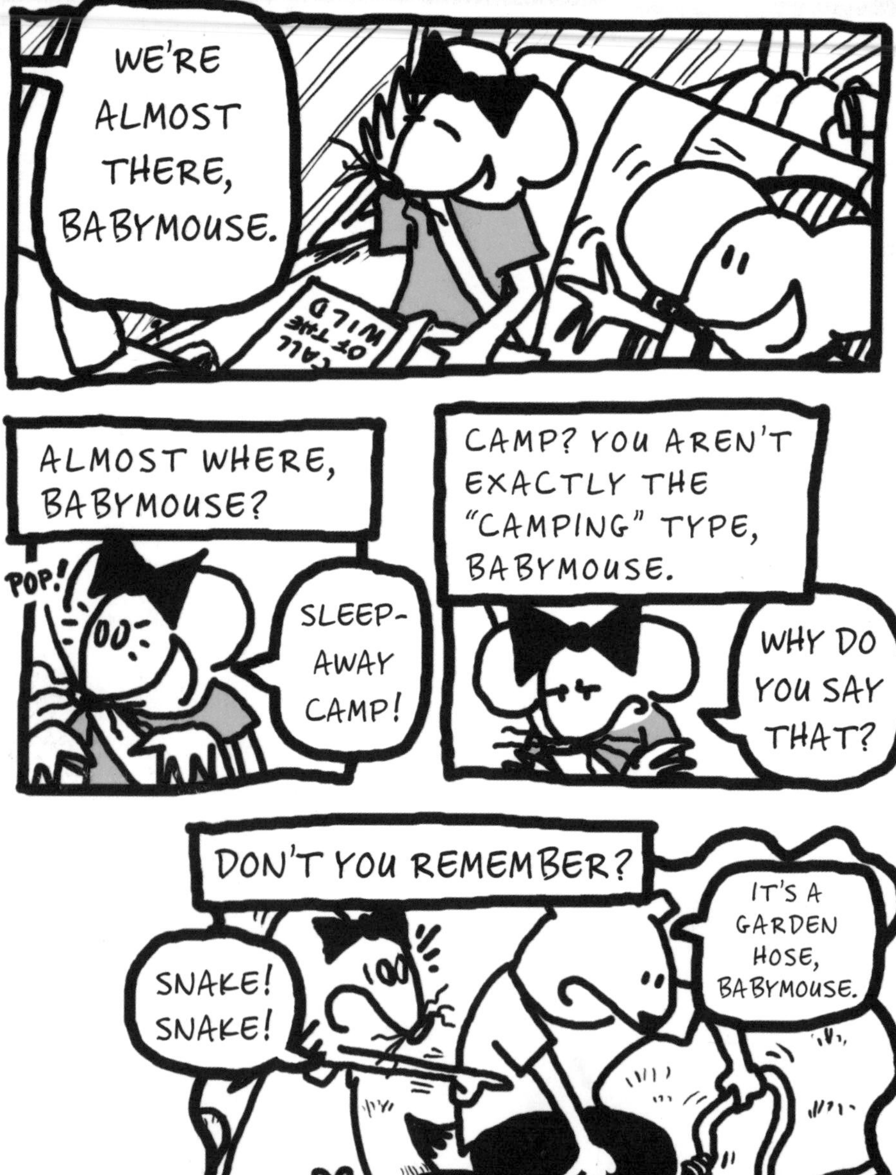
WE'RE ALMOST THERE, BABYMOUSE.
CALL OF THE WILD
ALMOST WHERE, BABYMOUSE?
POP!
SLEEP-AWAY CAMP!
CAMP? YOU AREN'T EXACTLY THE "CAMPING" TYPE, BABYMOUSE.
WHY DO YOU SAY THAT?
DON'T YOU REMEMBER?
SNAKE! SNAKE!
IT'S A GARDEN HOSE, BABYMOUSE.

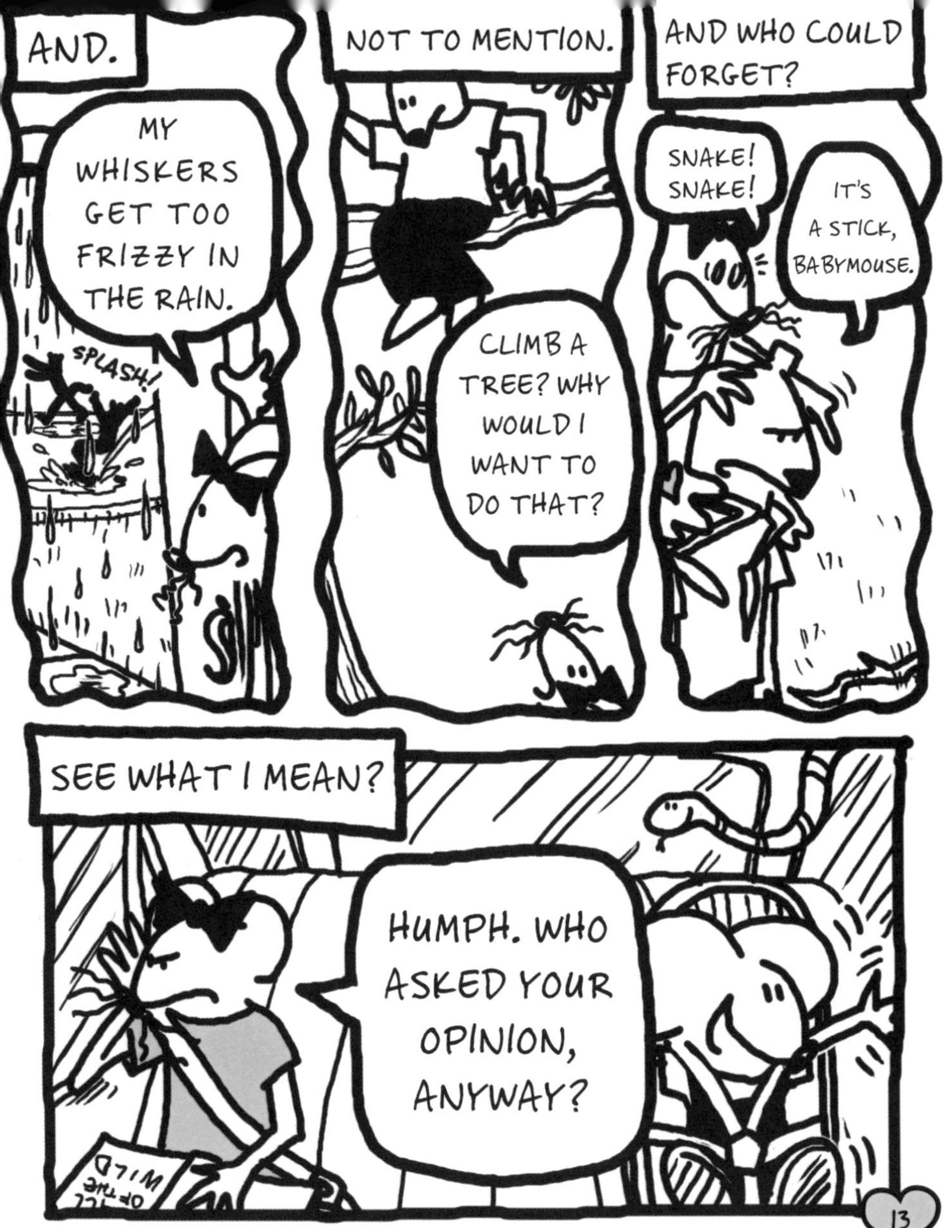
AND.
MY WHISKERS GET TOO FRIZZY IN THE RAIN.
SPLASH!
NOT TO MENTION.
CLIMB A TREE? WHY WOULD I WANT TO DO THAT?
AND WHO COULD FORGET?
SNAKE! SNAKE!
IT'S A STICK, BABYMOUSE.
SEE WHAT I MEAN?
HUMPH. WHO ASKED YOUR OPINION, ANYWAY?

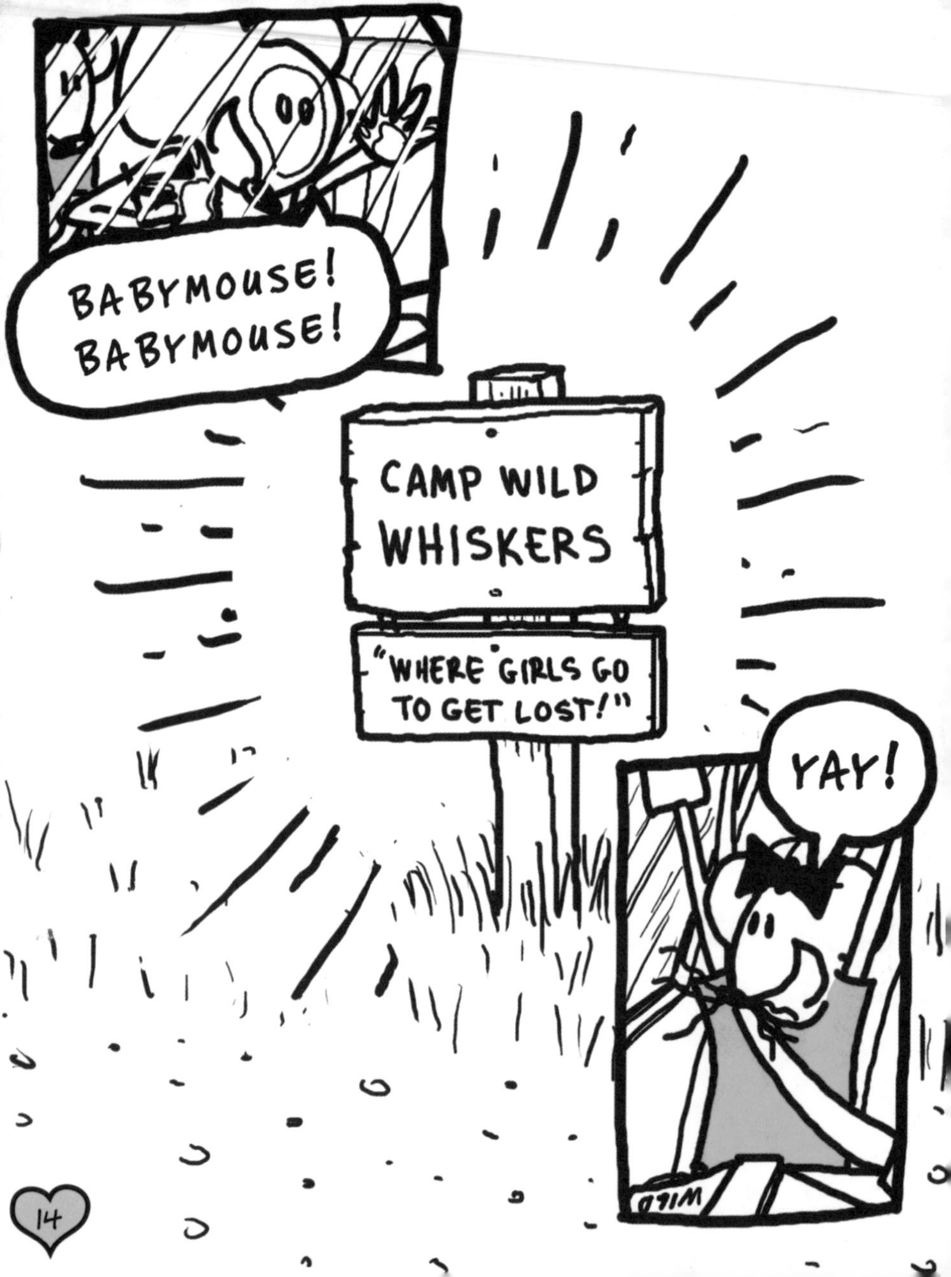
BABYMOUSE! BABYMOUSE!
CAMP WILD WHISKERS
"WHERE GIRLS GO TO GET LOST!"
YAY!

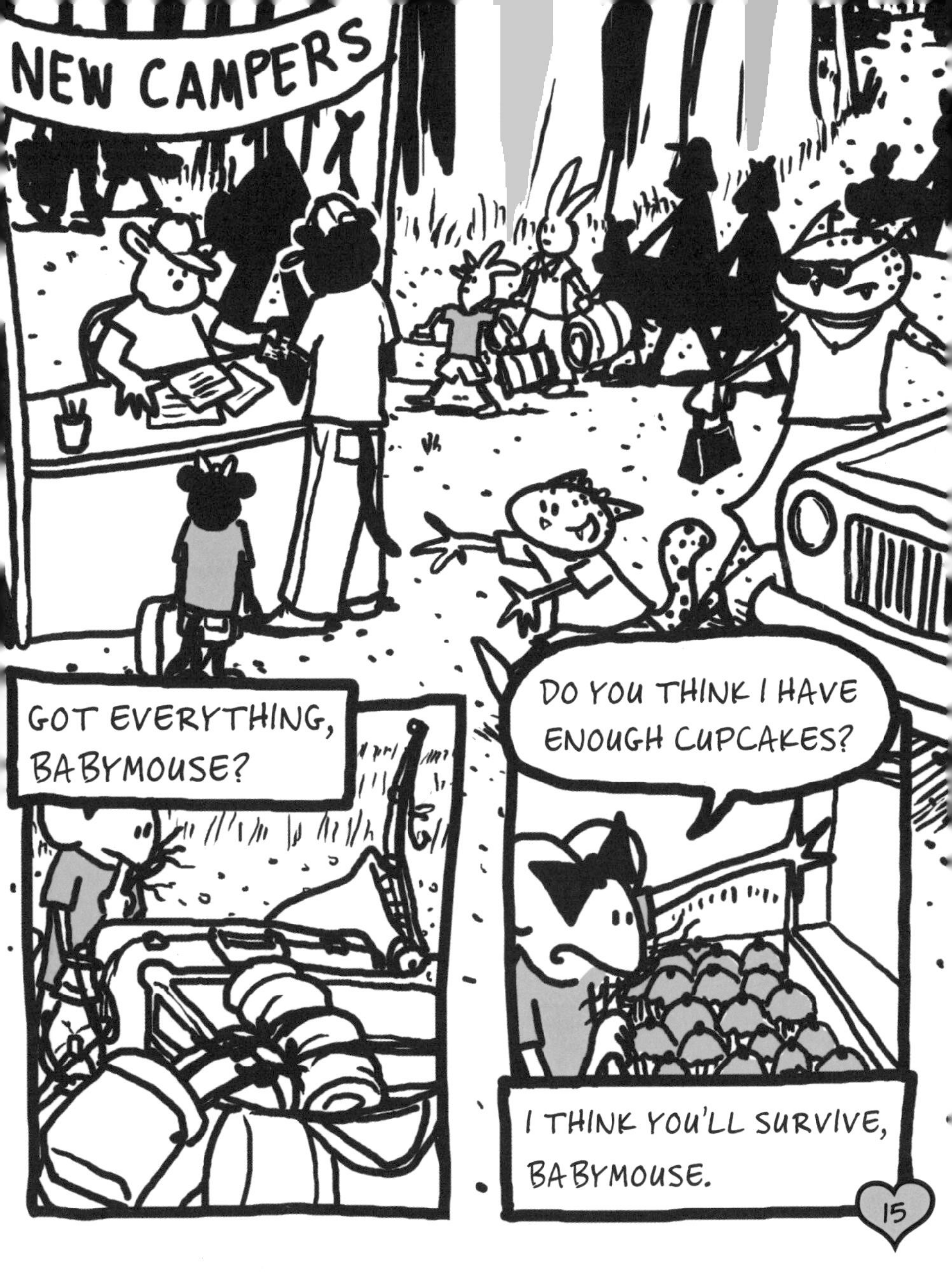
NEW CAMPERS
GOT EVERYTHING, BABYMOUSE?
DO YOU THINK I HAVE ENOUGH CUPCAKES?
I THINK YOU'LL SURVIVE, BABYMOUSE.

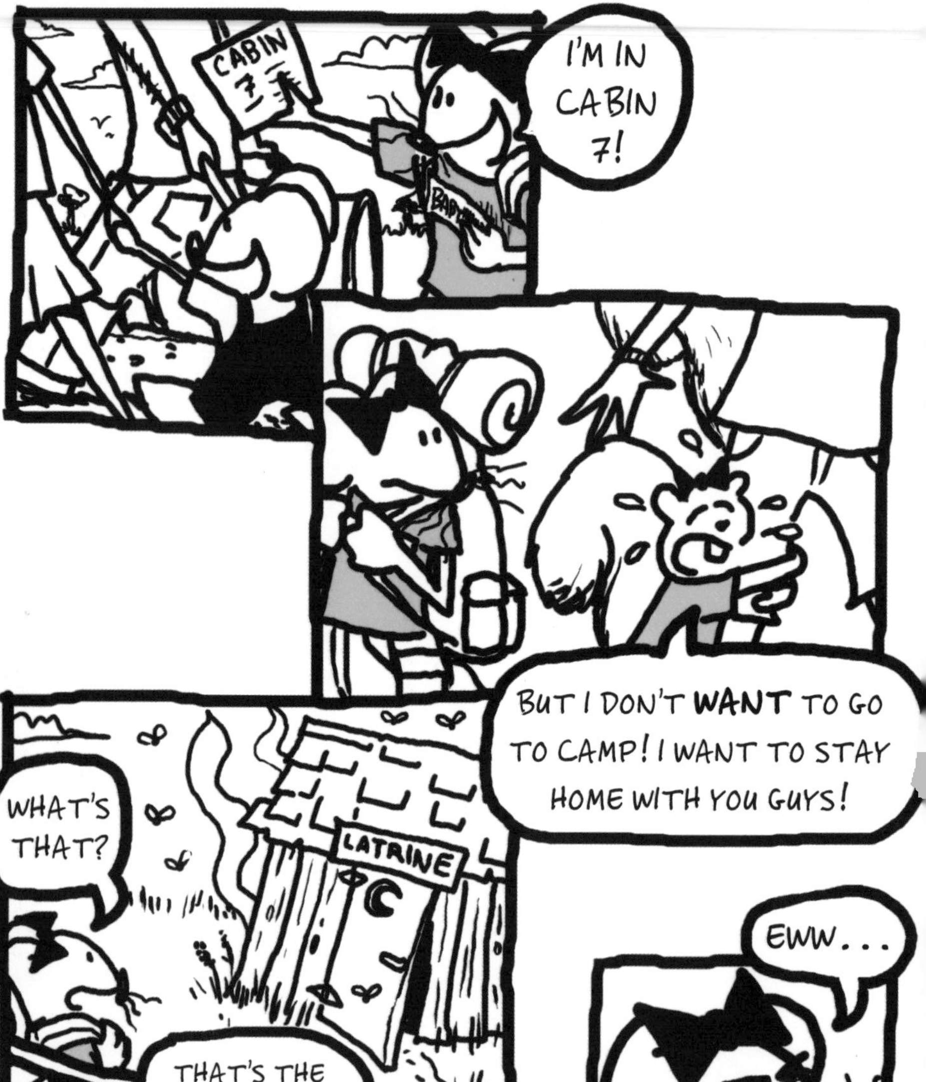
CABIN 7
I'M IN CABIN 7!
BUT I DON'T **WANT** TO GO TO CAMP! I WANT TO STAY HOME WITH YOU GUYS!
WHAT'S THAT?
LATRINE
THAT'S THE BATHROOM, BABYMOUSE.
EWW...

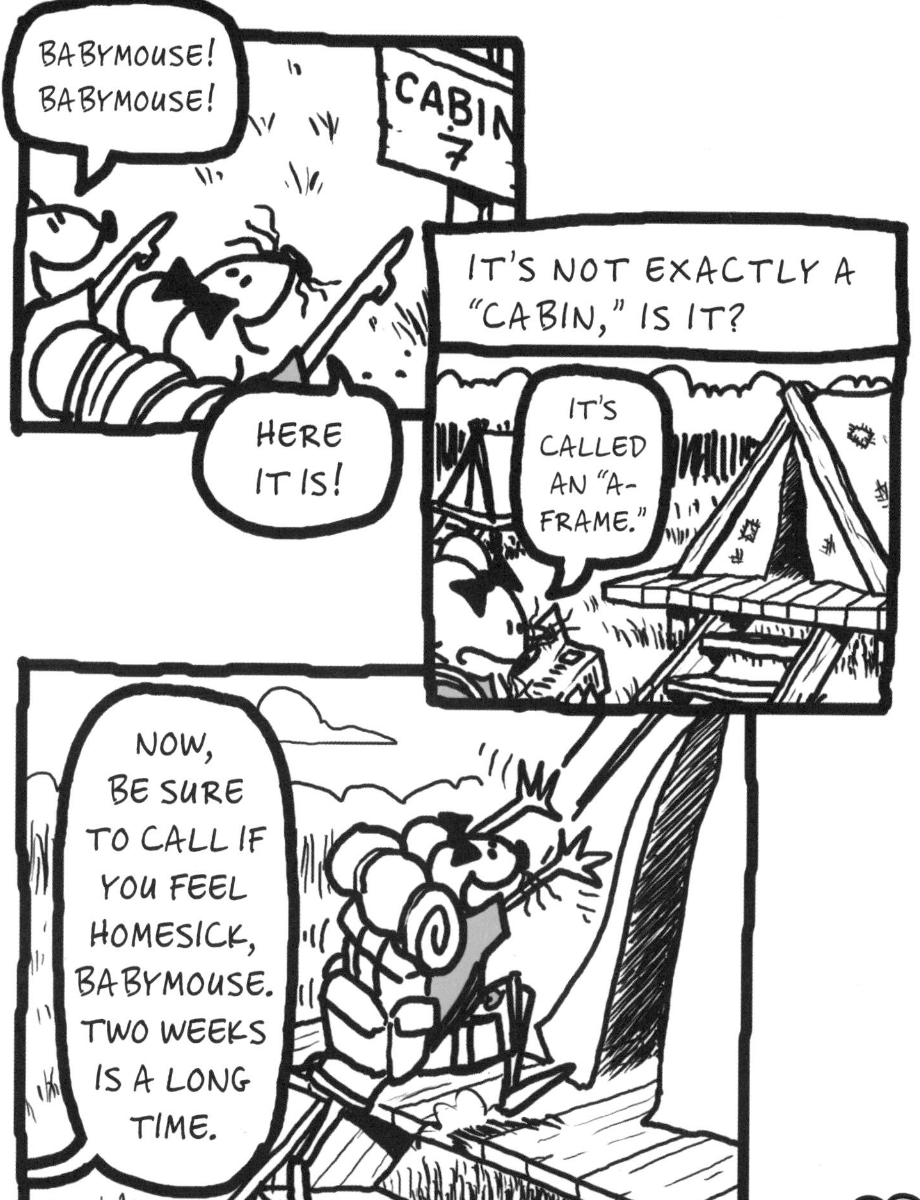
BABYMOUSE! BABYMOUSE!
CABIN 7
HERE IT IS!
IT'S NOT EXACTLY A "CABIN," IS IT?
IT'S CALLED AN "A-FRAME."
NOW, BE SURE TO CALL IF YOU FEEL HOMESICK, BABYMOUSE. TWO WEEKS IS A LONG TIME.

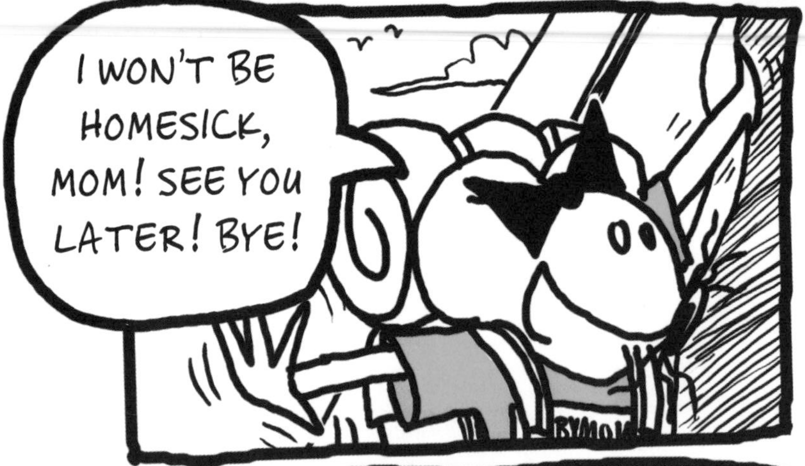
I WON'T BE HOMESICK, MOM! SEE YOU LATER! BYE!
BABYMOUSE

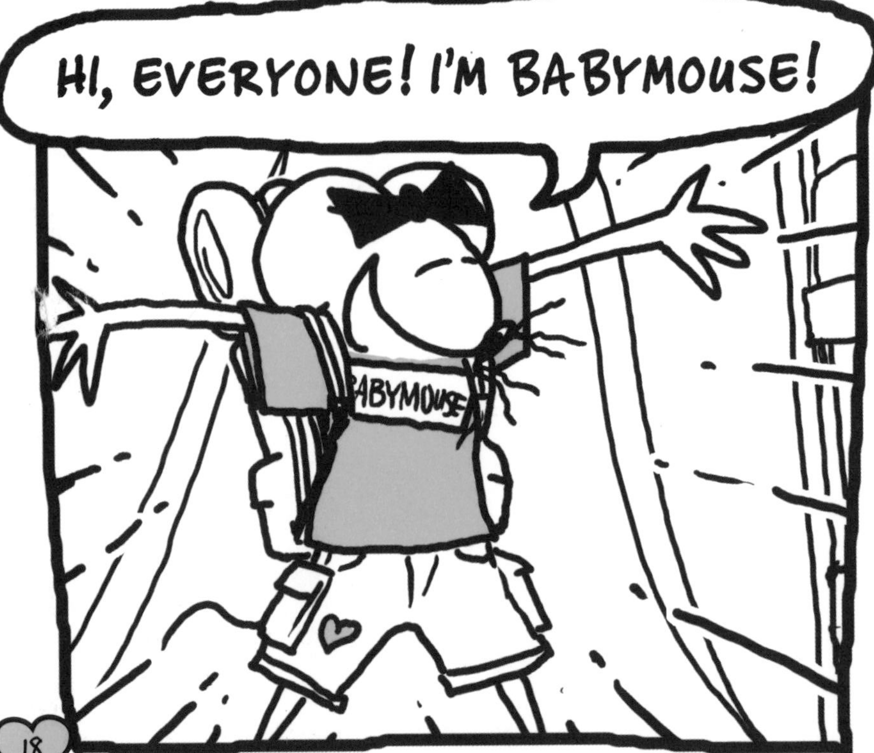
HI, EVERYONE! I'M BABYMOUSE!
BABYMOUSE

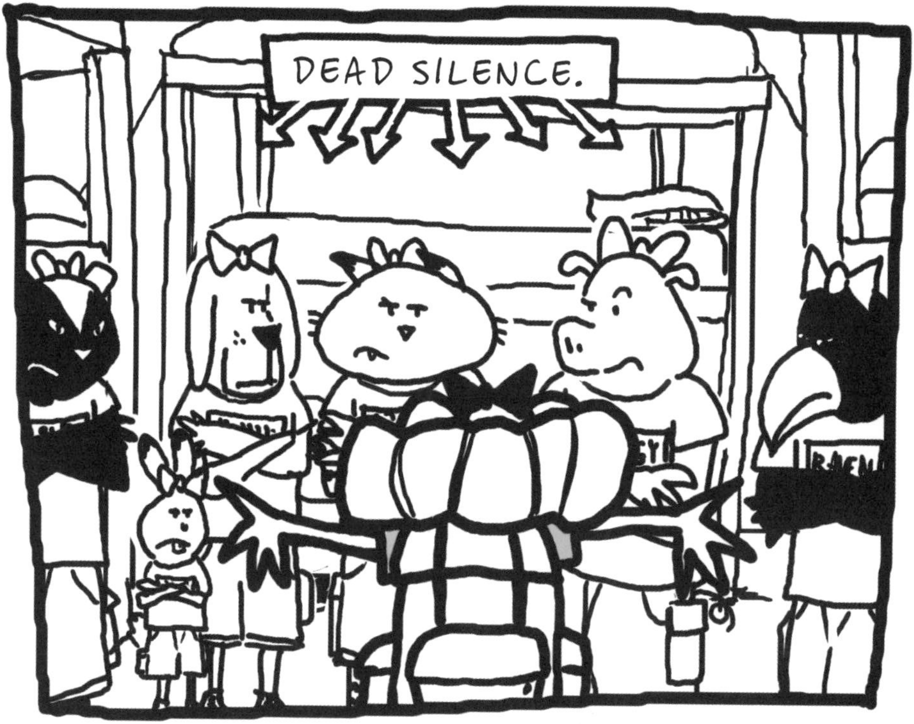
DEAD SILENCE.

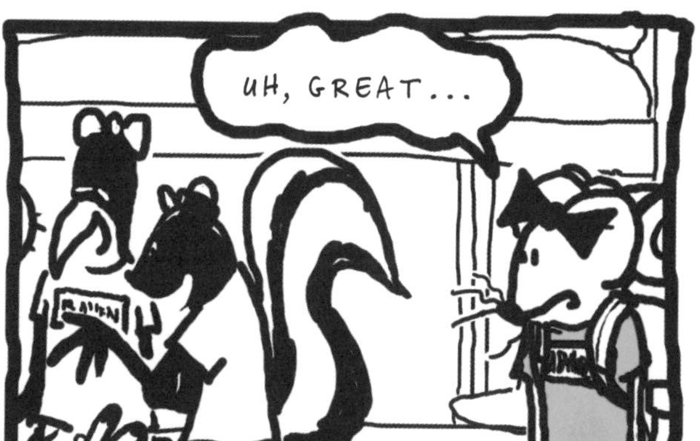
UH, GREAT...

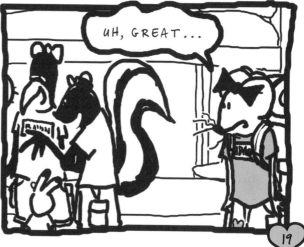

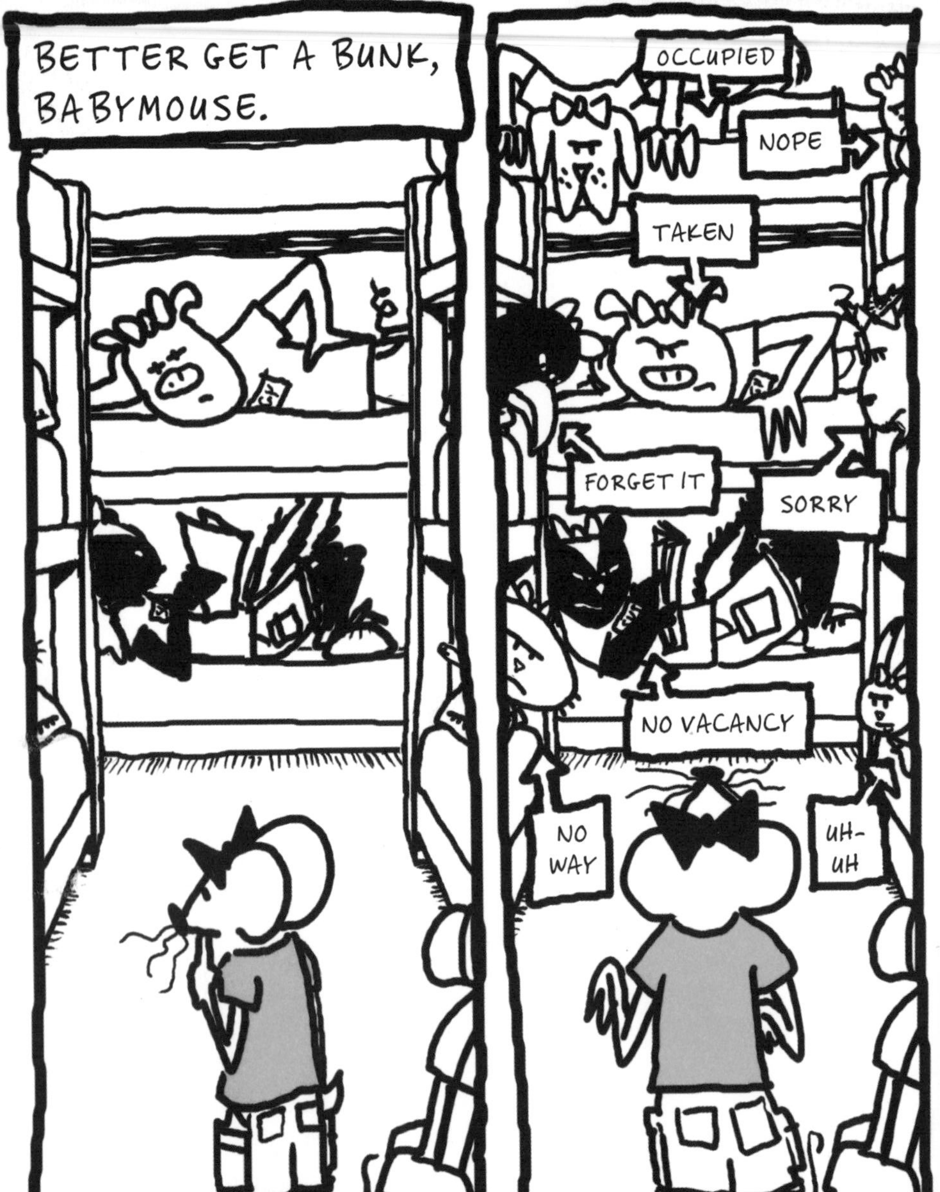
BETTER GET A BUNK, BABYMOUSE.
OCCUPIED
NOPE
TAKEN
FORGET IT
SORRY
NO VACANCY
NO WAY
UH-UH

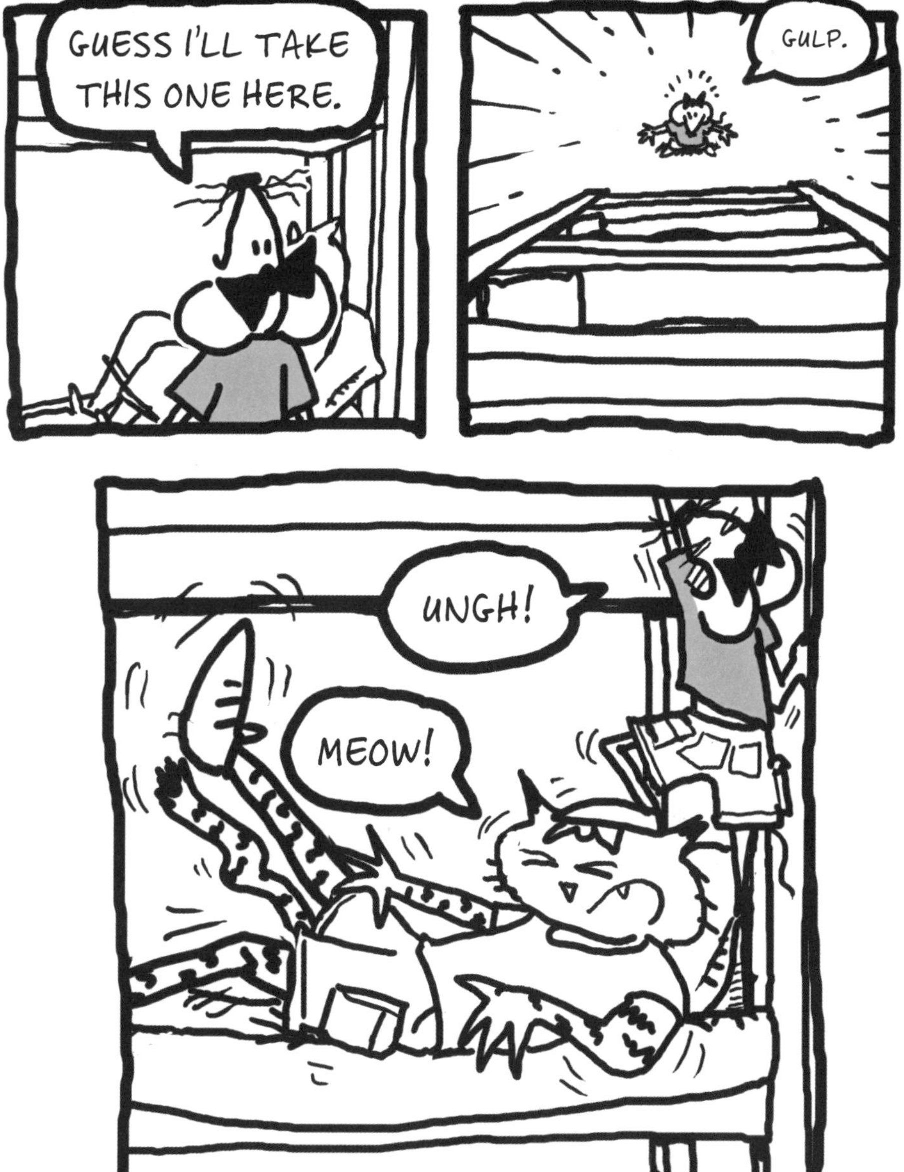
GUESS I'LL TAKE THIS ONE HERE.
GULP.
UNGH!
MEOW!

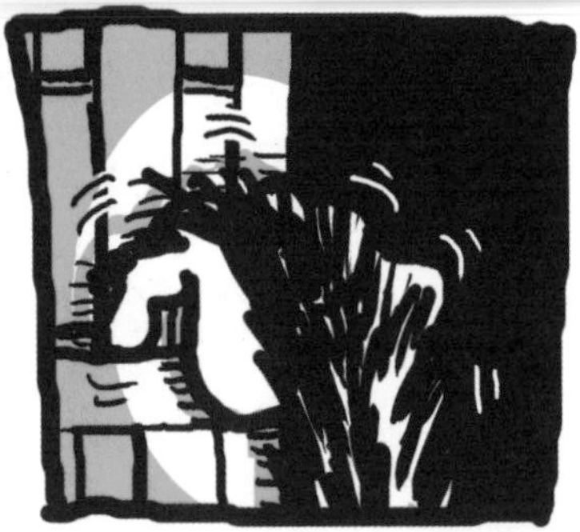

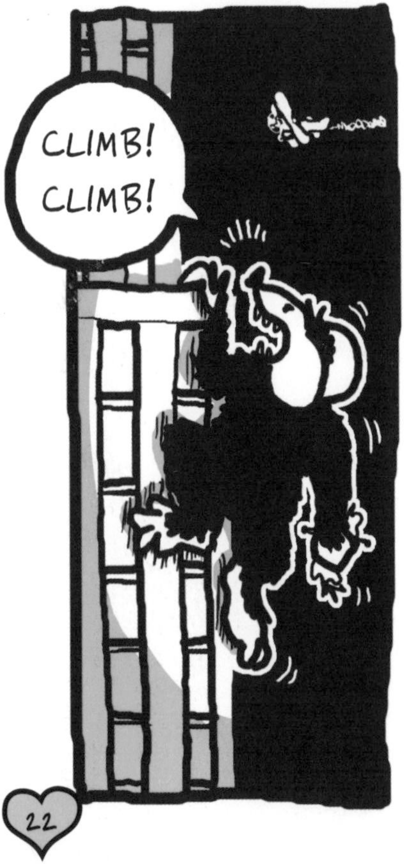
CLIMB!
CLIMB!

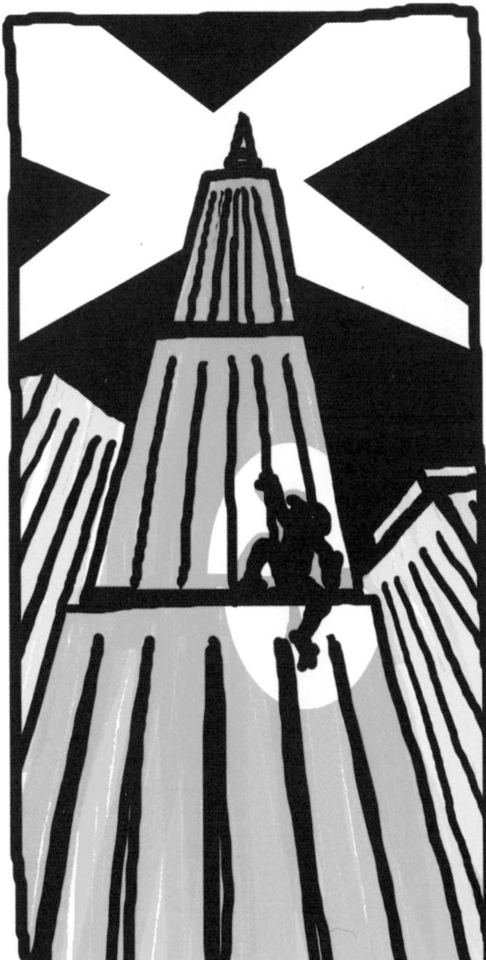

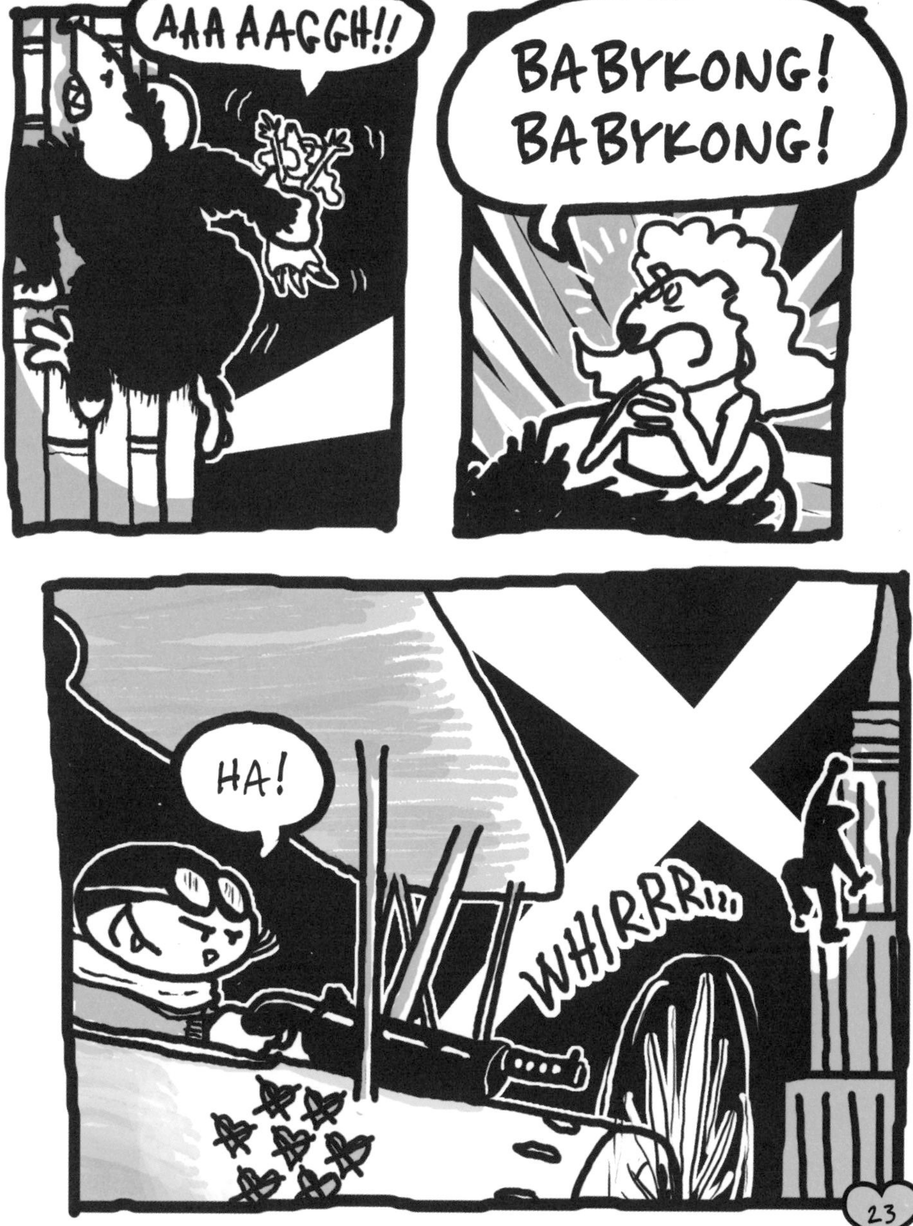
AAA AAGGH!!
BABYKONG! BABYKONG!
HA!
WHIRRR...

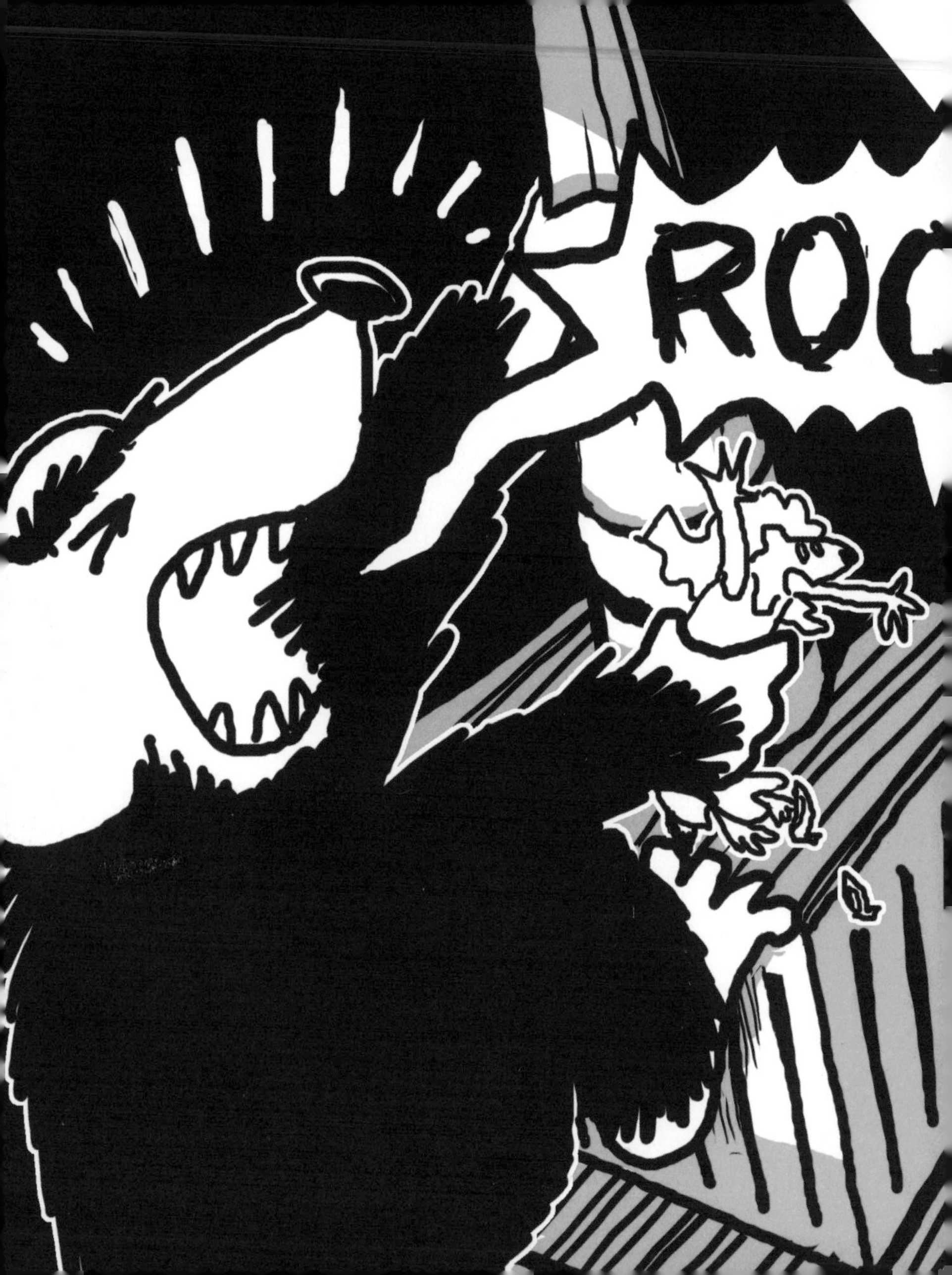
ROO

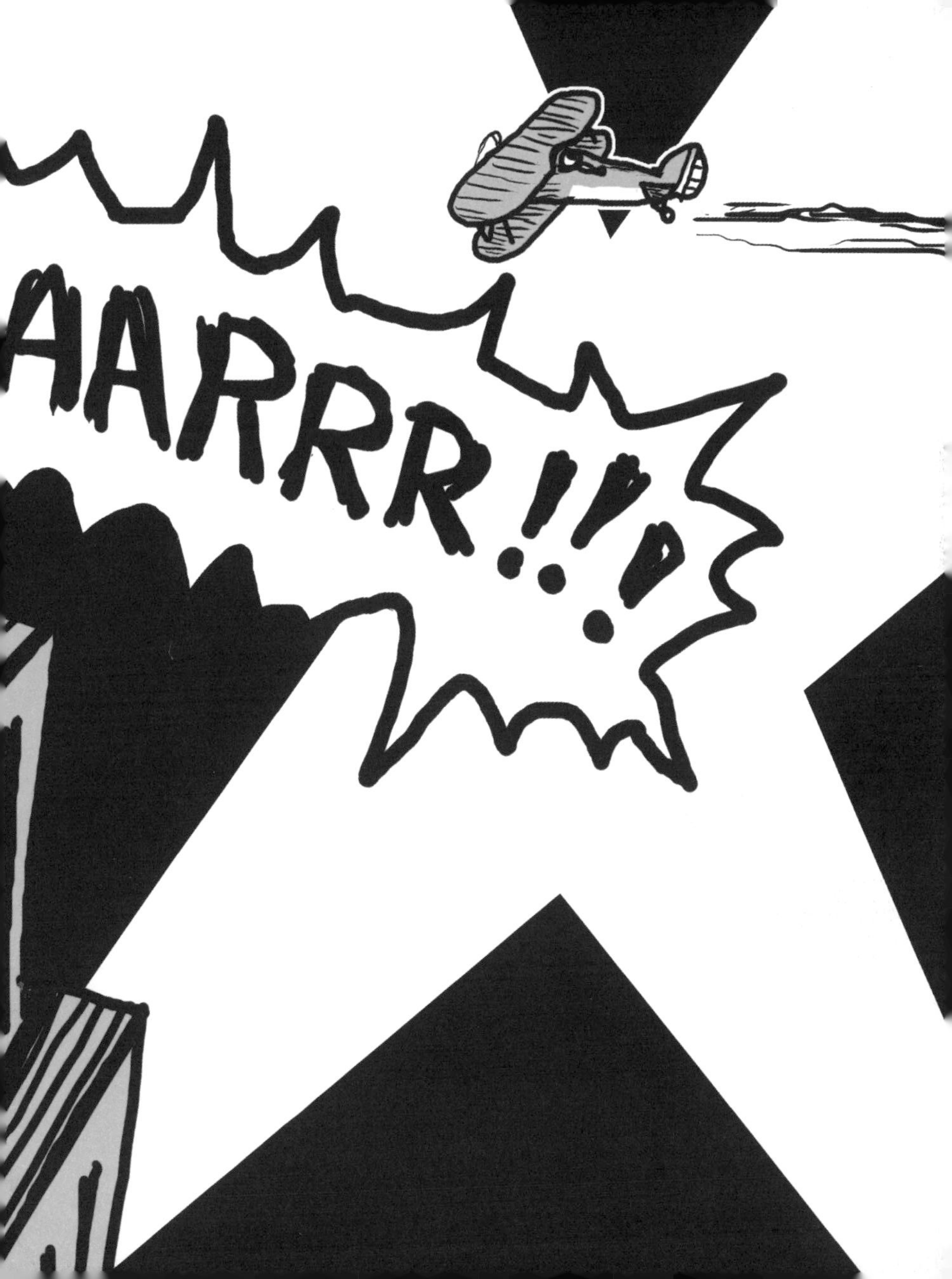
AARRRR!!!

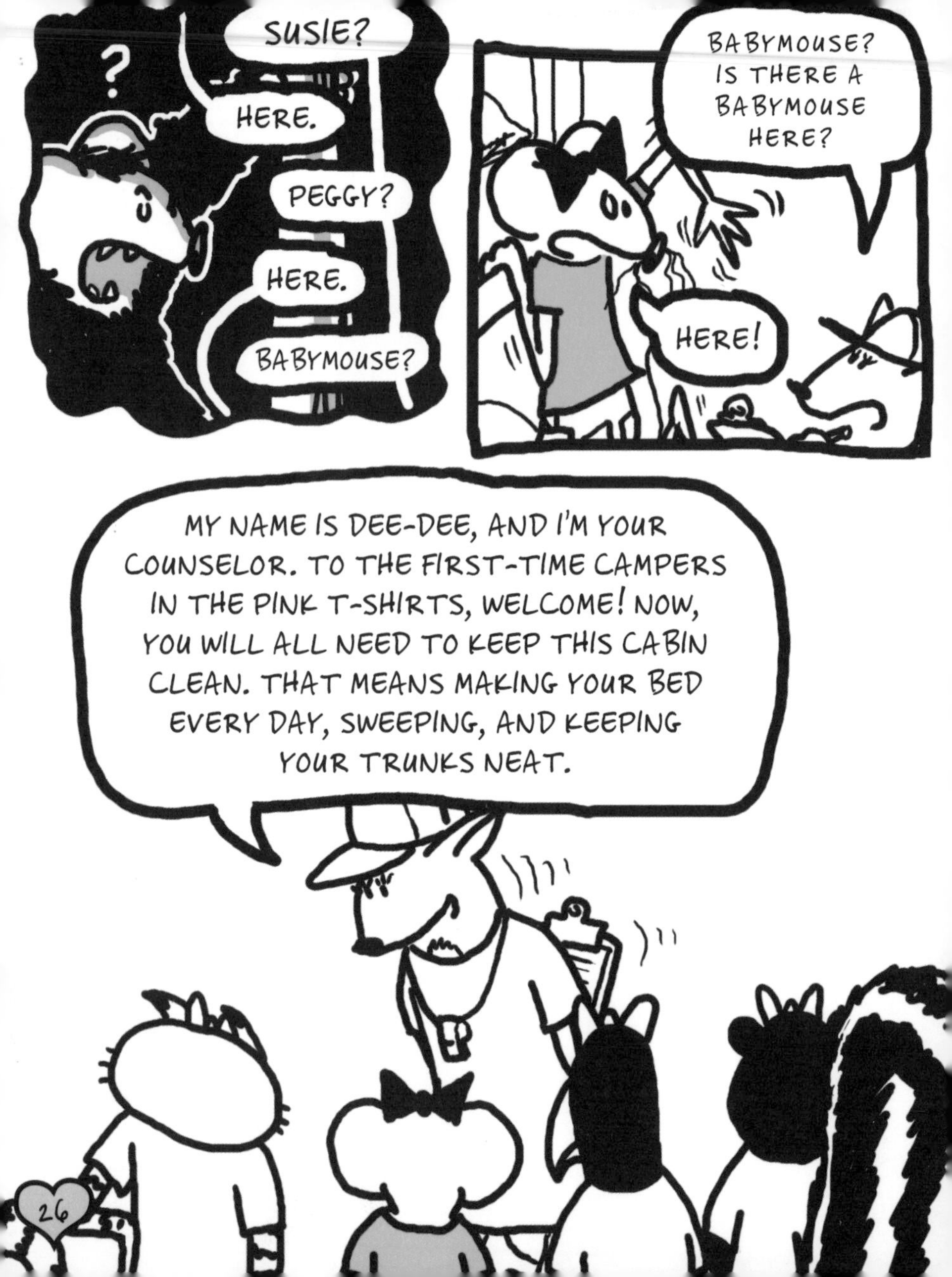
SUSIE?
HERE.
PEGGY?
HERE.
BABYMOUSE?
BABYMOUSE? IS THERE A BABYMOUSE HERE?
HERE!
MY NAME IS DEE-DEE, AND I'M YOUR COUNSELOR. TO THE FIRST-TIME CAMPERS IN THE PINK T-SHIRTS, WELCOME! NOW, YOU WILL ALL NEED TO KEEP THIS CABIN CLEAN. THAT MEANS MAKING YOUR BED EVERY DAY, SWEEPING, AND KEEPING YOUR TRUNKS NEAT.

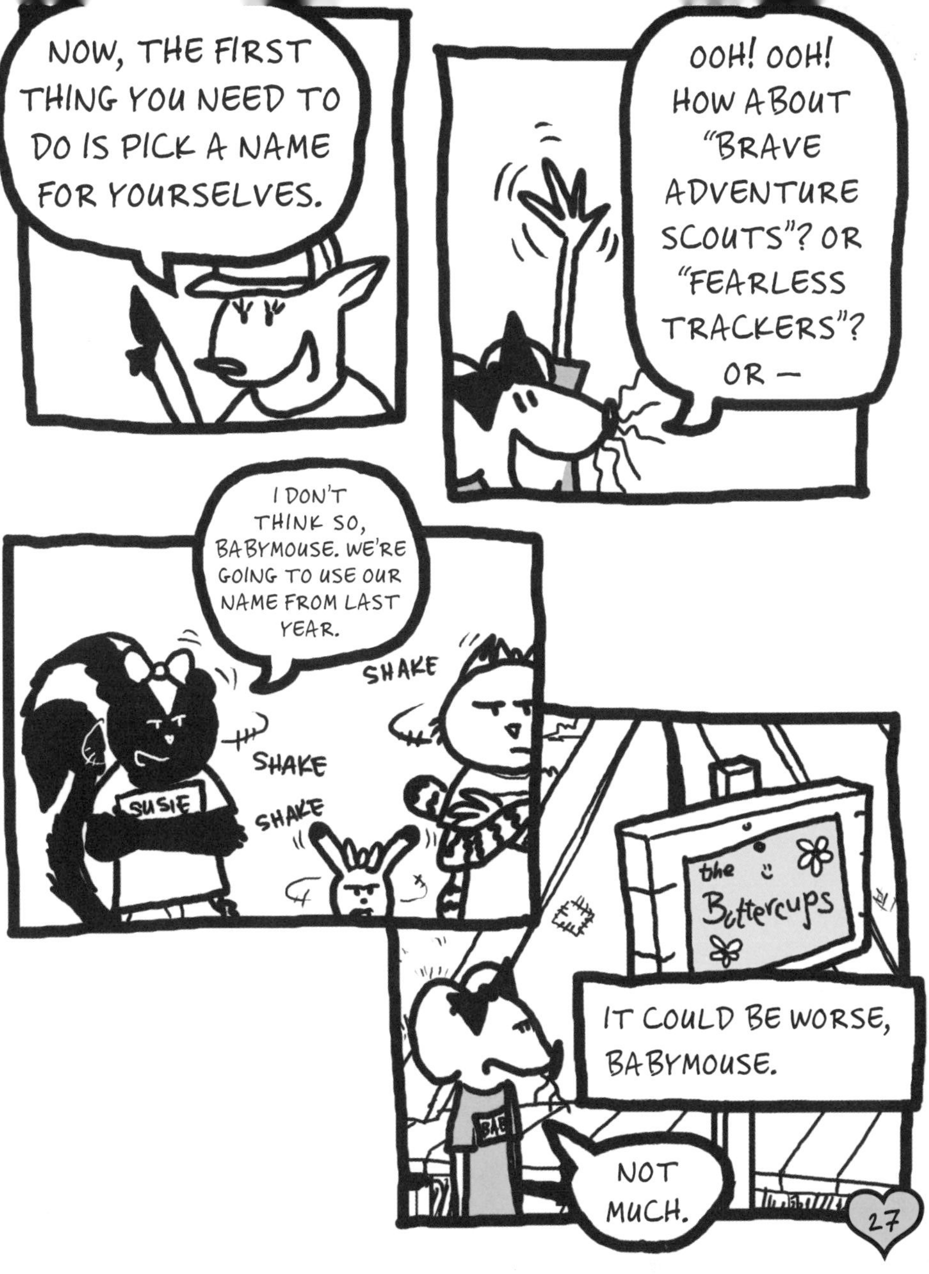

NOW, THE FIRST THING YOU NEED TO DO IS PICK A NAME FOR YOURSELVES.
OOH! OOH! HOW ABOUT "BRAVE ADVENTURE SCOUTS"? OR "FEARLESS TRACKERS"? OR —
I DON'T THINK SO, BABYMOUSE. WE'RE GOING TO USE OUR NAME FROM LAST YEAR.
SHAKE
SHAKE
SHAKE
SUSIE
the Buttercups
IT COULD BE WORSE, BABYMOUSE.
NOT MUCH.

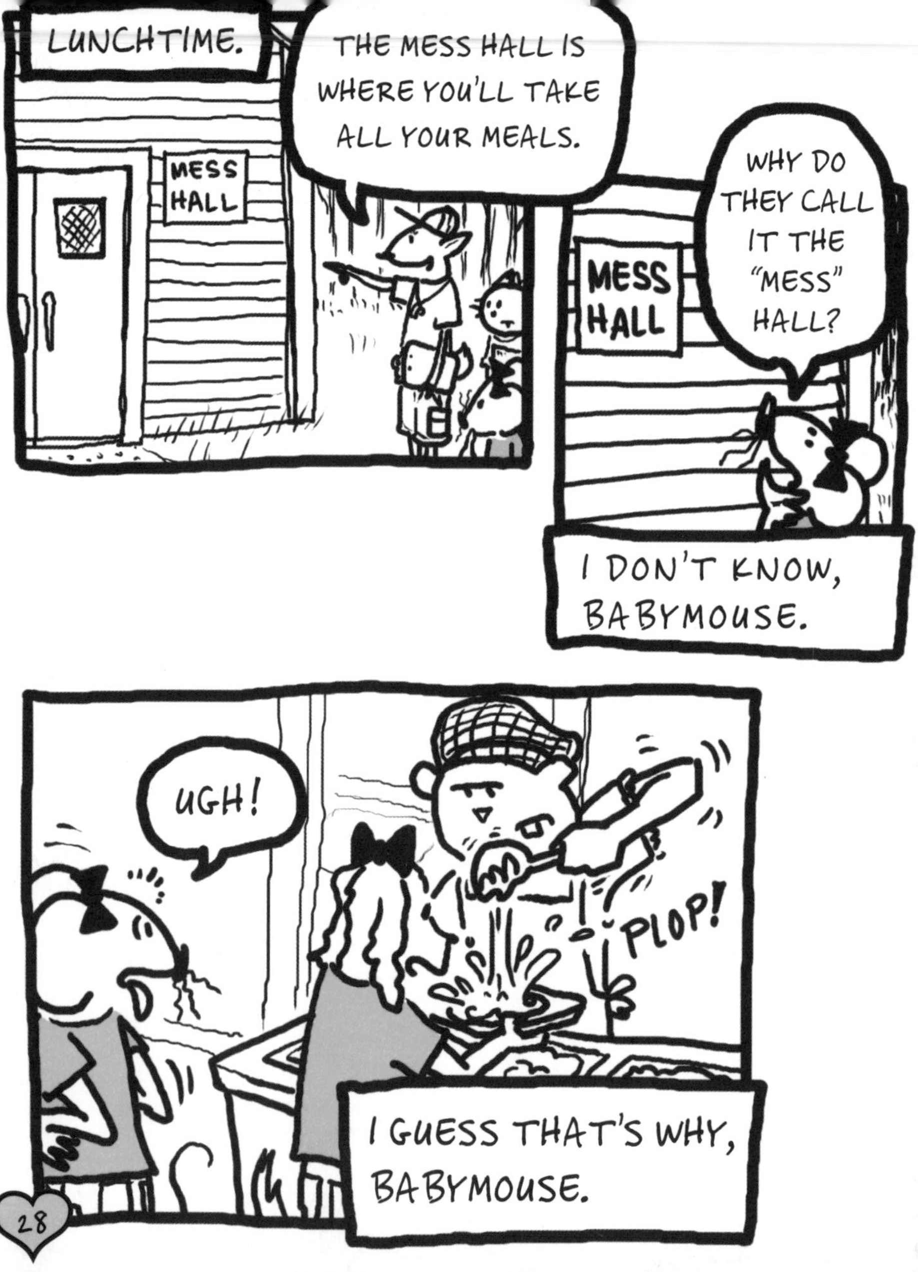
LUNCHTIME.
THE MESS HALL IS WHERE YOU'LL TAKE ALL YOUR MEALS.
MESS HALL
MESS HALL
WHY DO THEY CALL IT THE "MESS" HALL?
I DON'T KNOW, BABYMOUSE.
UGH!
PLOP!
I GUESS THAT'S WHY, BABYMOUSE.

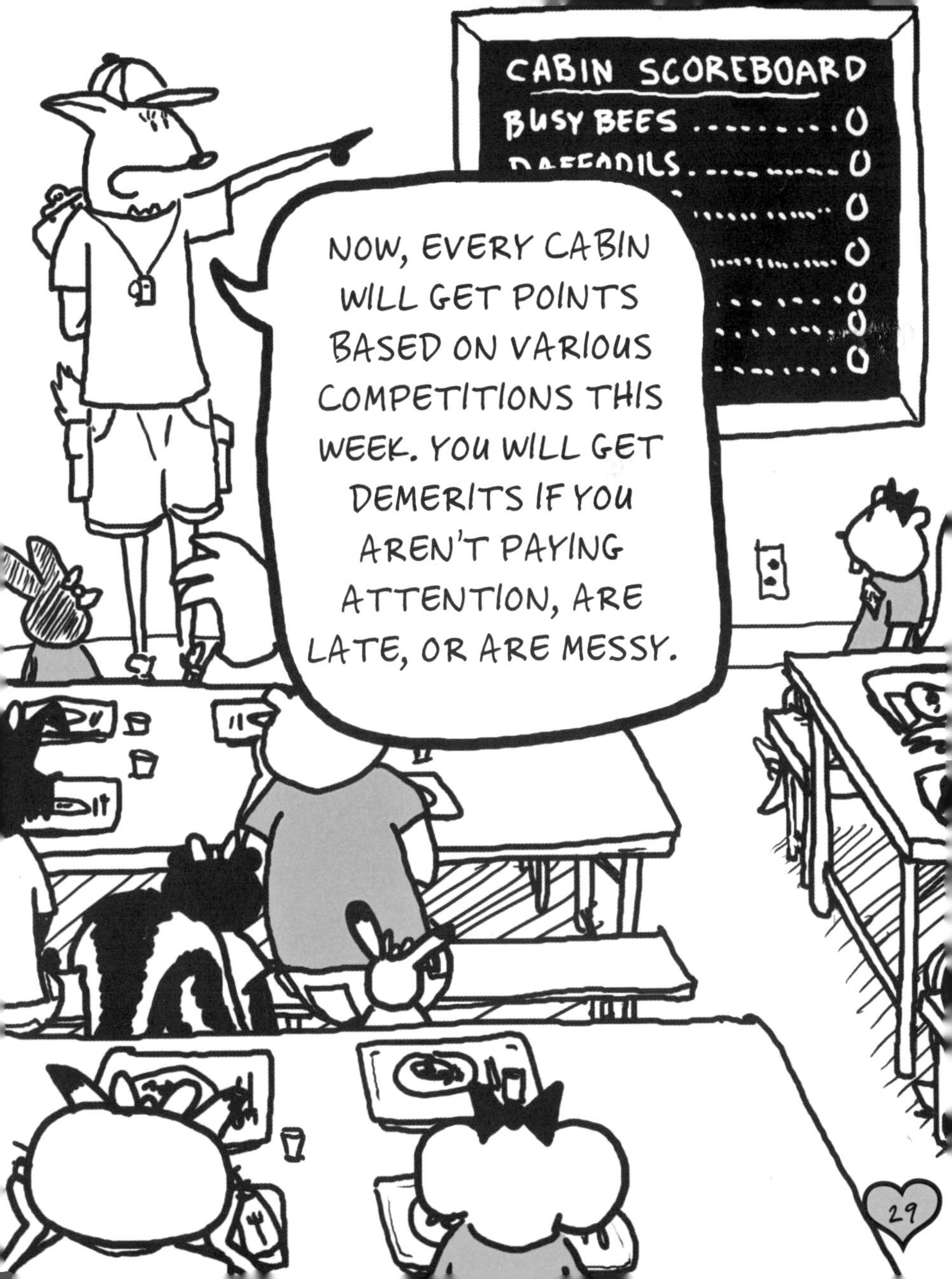
CABIN SCOREBOARD
BUSY BEES 0
0
0
0
0
0
0
NOW, EVERY CABIN WILL GET POINTS BASED ON VARIOUS COMPETITIONS THIS WEEK. YOU WILL GET DEMERITS IF YOU AREN'T PAYING ATTENTION, ARE LATE, OR ARE MESSY.

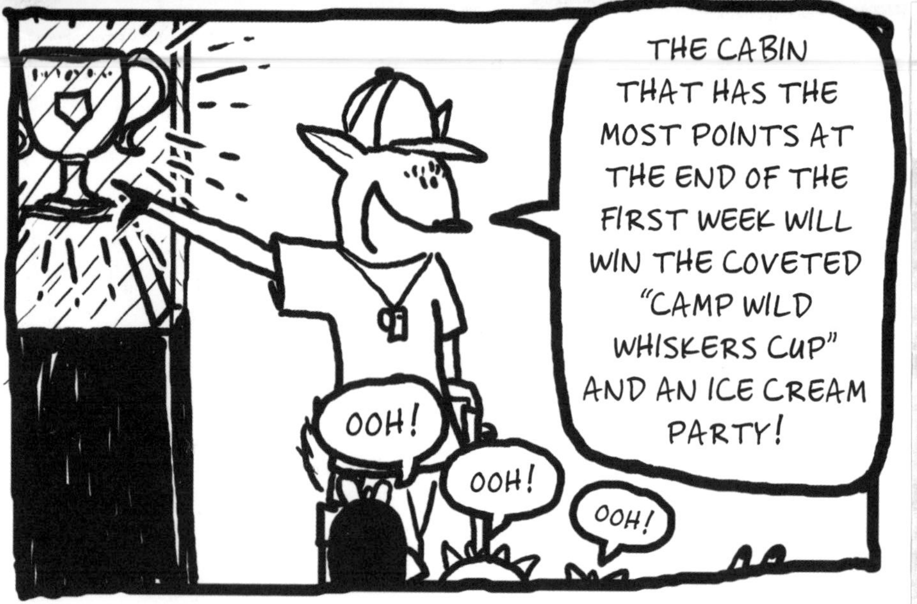
THE CABIN THAT HAS THE MOST POINTS AT THE END OF THE FIRST WEEK WILL WIN THE COVETED "CAMP WILD WHISKERS CUP" AND AN ICE CREAM PARTY!
OOH!
OOH!
OOH!

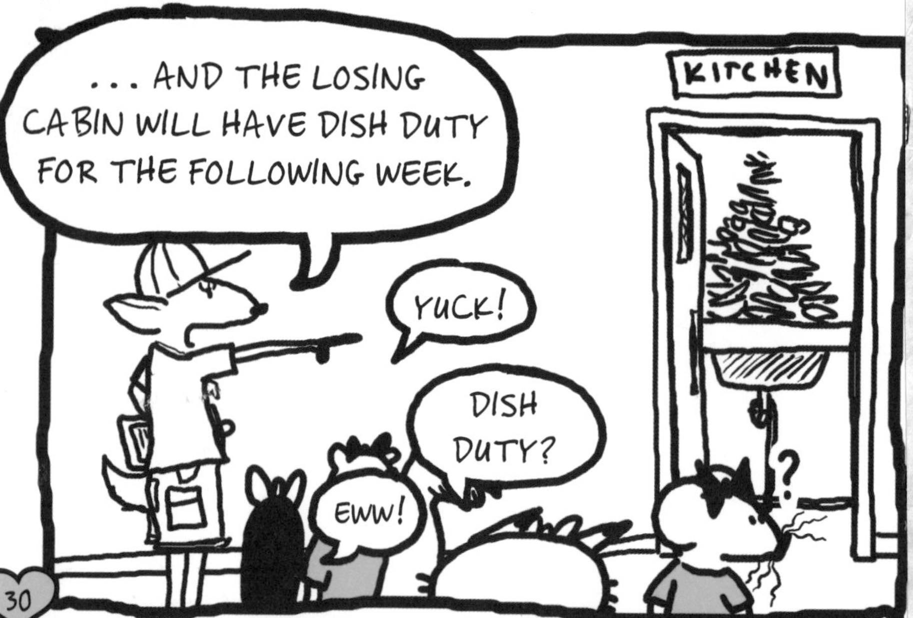
. . . AND THE LOSING CABIN WILL HAVE DISH DUTY FOR THE FOLLOWING WEEK.
KITCHEN
YUCK!
DISH DUTY?
EWW!
?

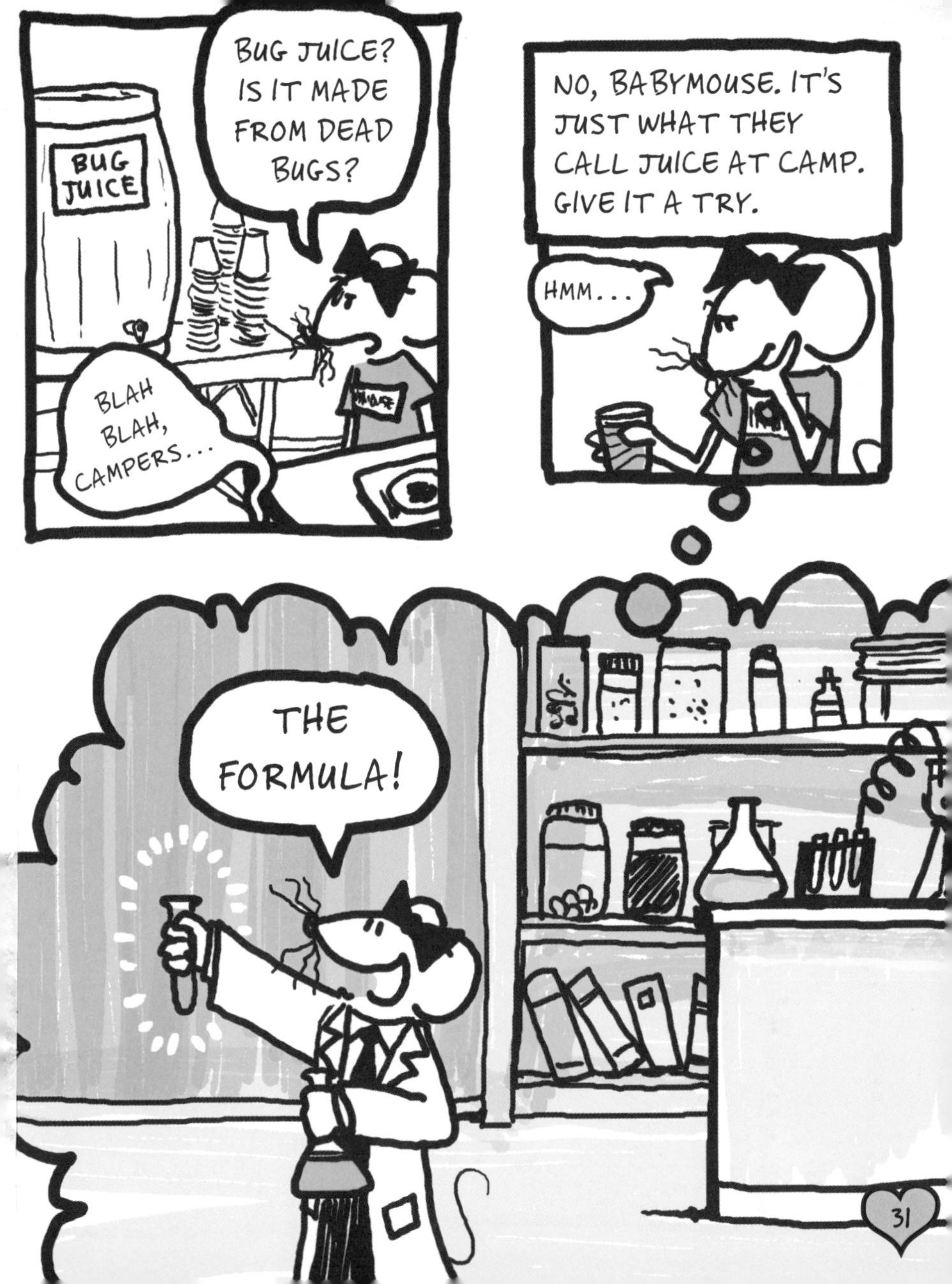
BUG JUICE
BUG JUICE? IS IT MADE FROM DEAD BUGS?
BLAH BLAH, CAMPERS...
NO, BABYMOUSE. IT'S JUST WHAT THEY CALL JUICE AT CAMP. GIVE IT A TRY.
HMM...
THE FORMULA!

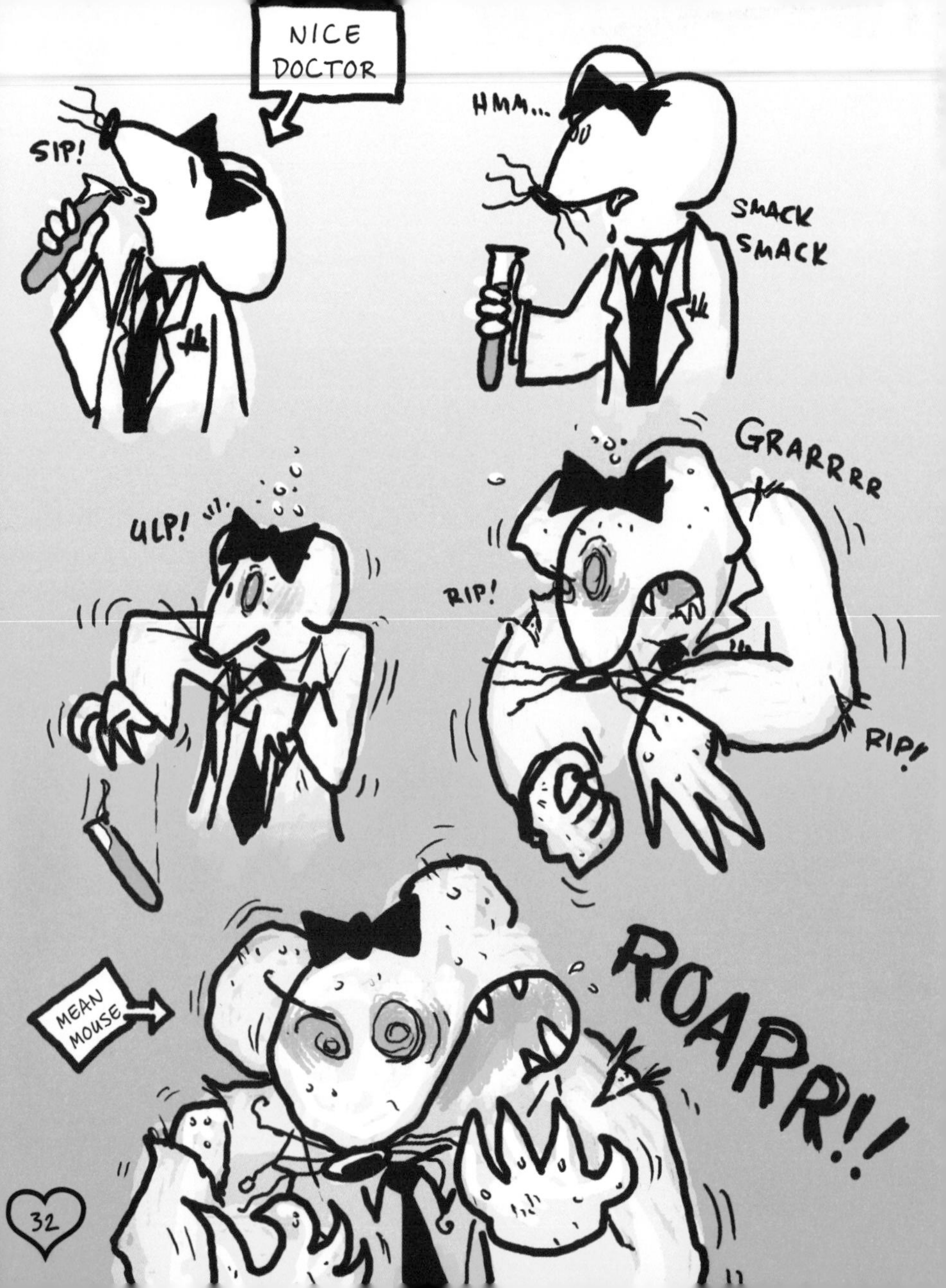
NICE DOCTOR
SIP!
HMM...
SMACK SMACK
ULP!
GRARRRRR
RIP!
RIP!
MEAN MOUSE
ROARR!!

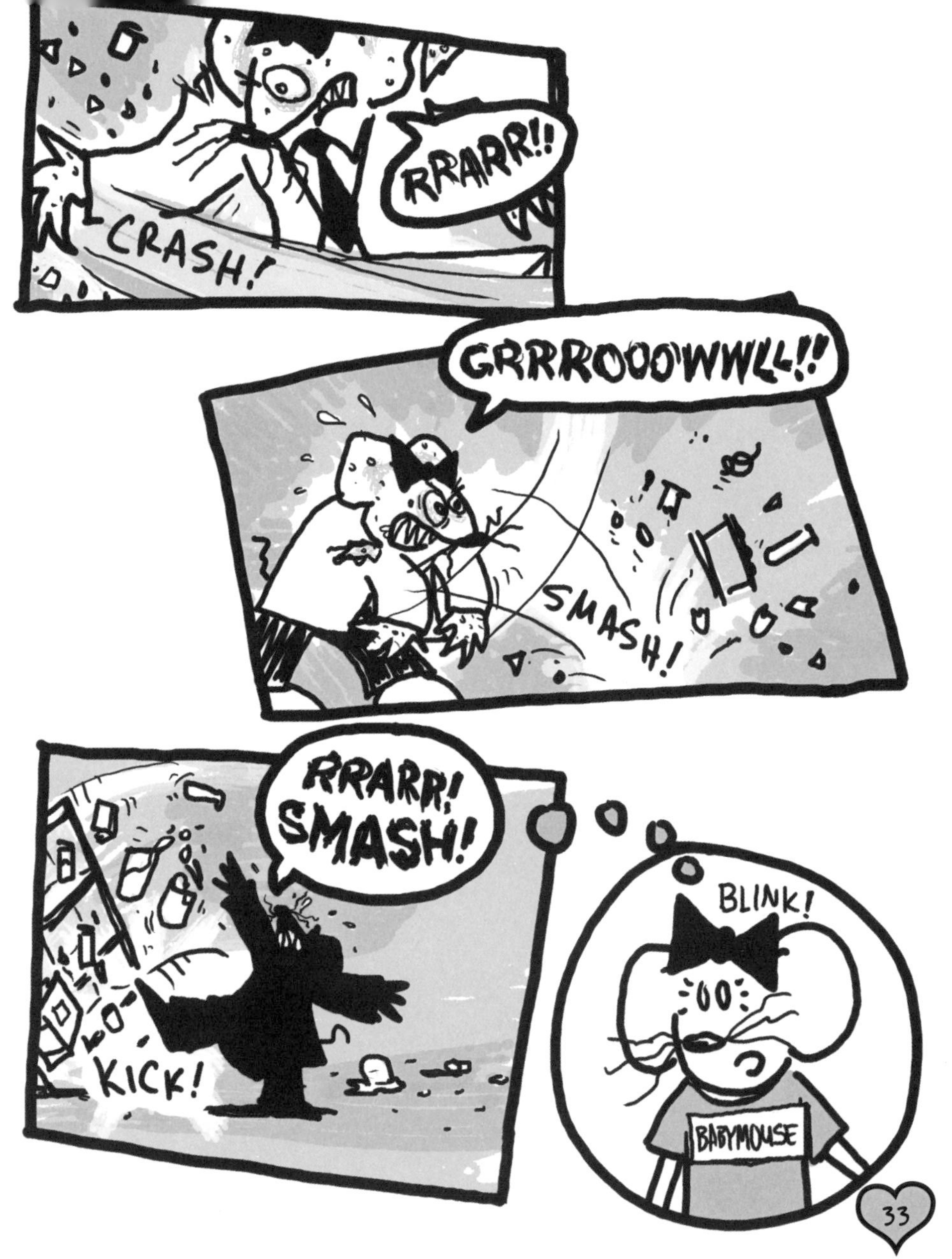
RRARR!!
CRASH!
GRRROOOWWLL!!
SMASH!
RRARR! SMASH!
KICK!
BLINK!
BABYMOUSE

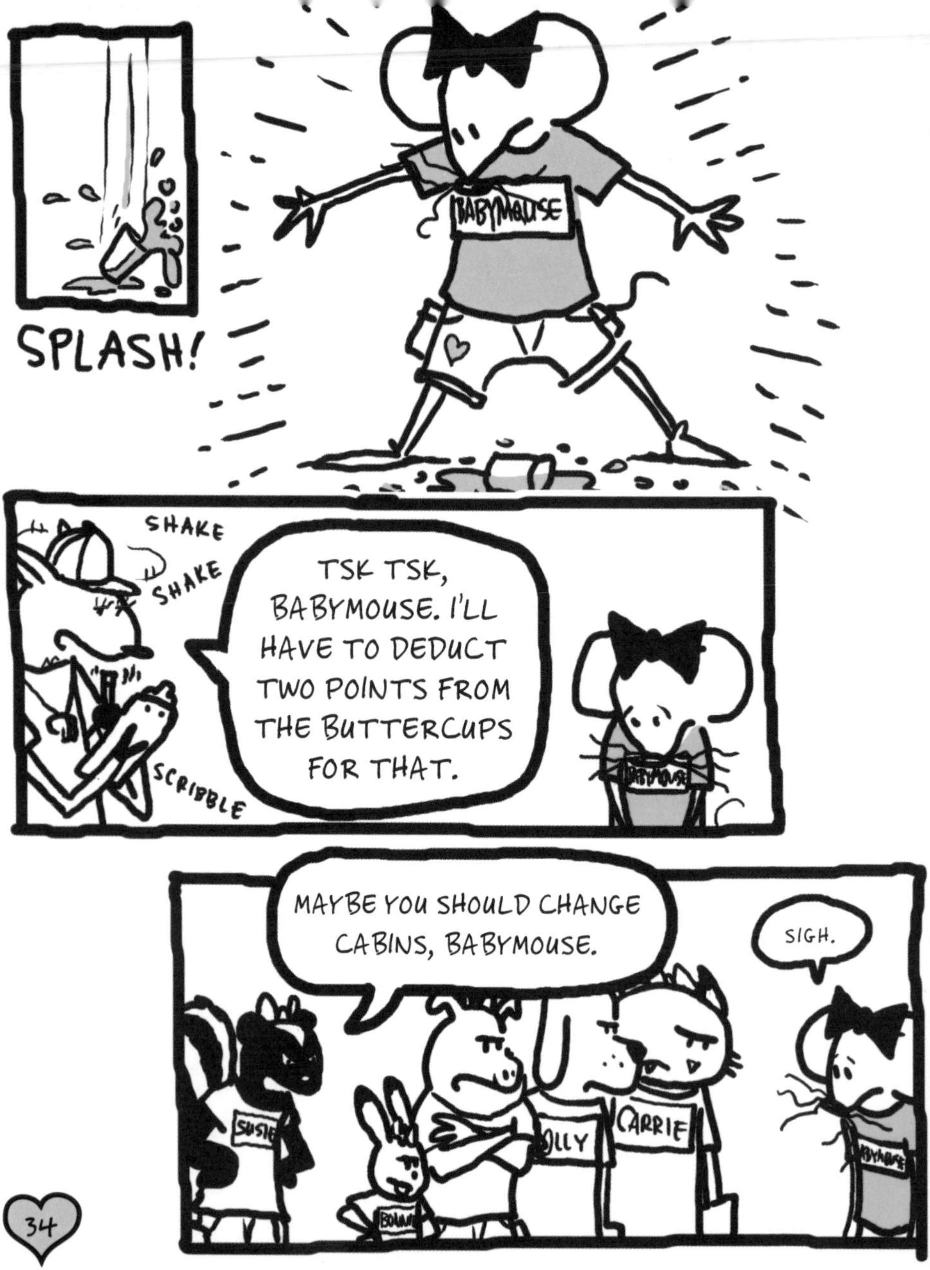
SPLASH!
BABYMOUSE
SHAKE
SHAKE
TSK TSK, BABYMOUSE. I'LL HAVE TO DEDUCT TWO POINTS FROM THE BUTTERCUPS FOR THAT.
SCRIBBLE
MAYBE YOU SHOULD CHANGE CABINS, BABYMOUSE.
SIGH.
SUSIE
CARRIE

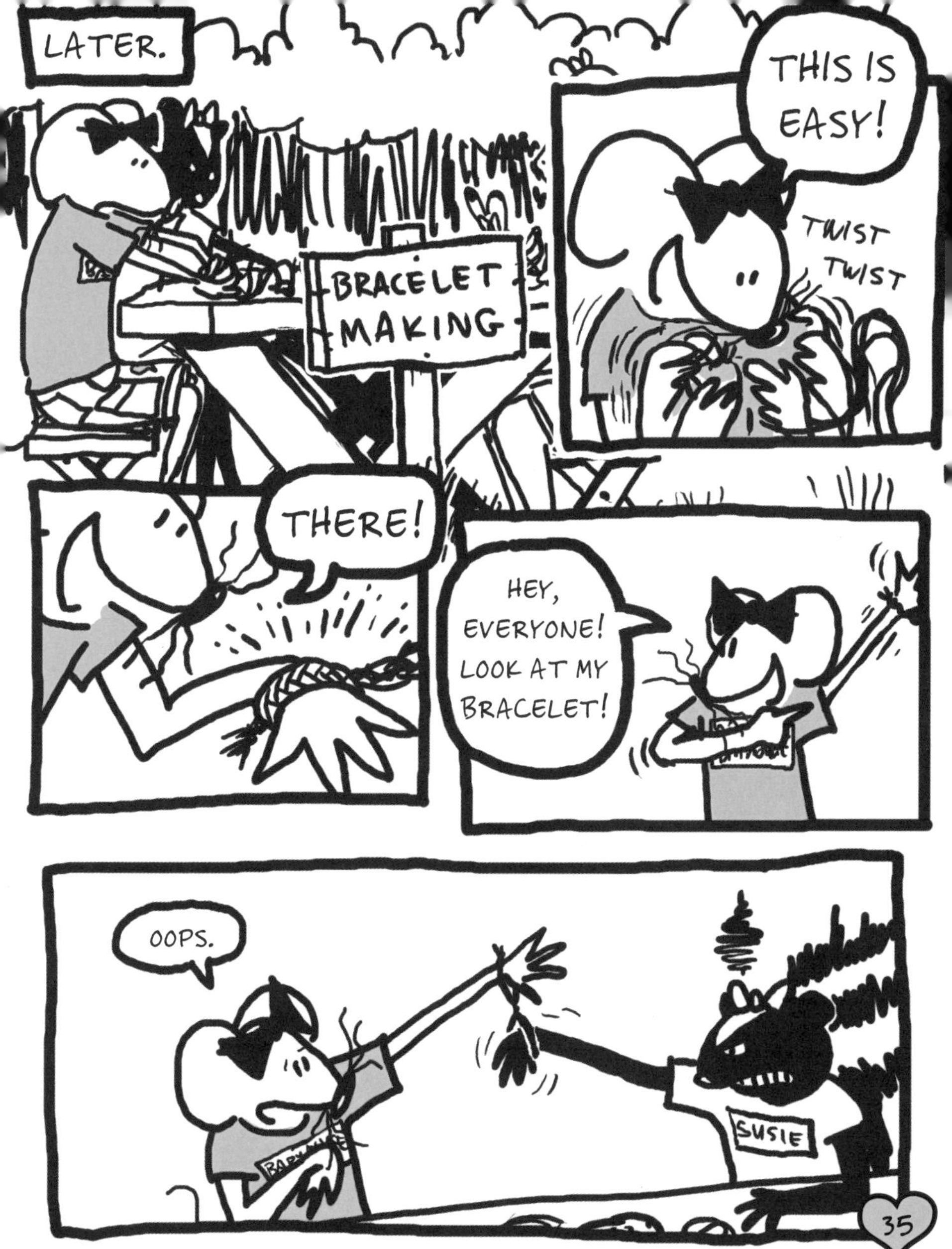
LATER.
BRACELET MAKING
THIS IS EASY!
TWIST TWIST
THERE!
HEY, EVERYONE! LOOK AT MY BRACELET!
OOPS.
SUSIE

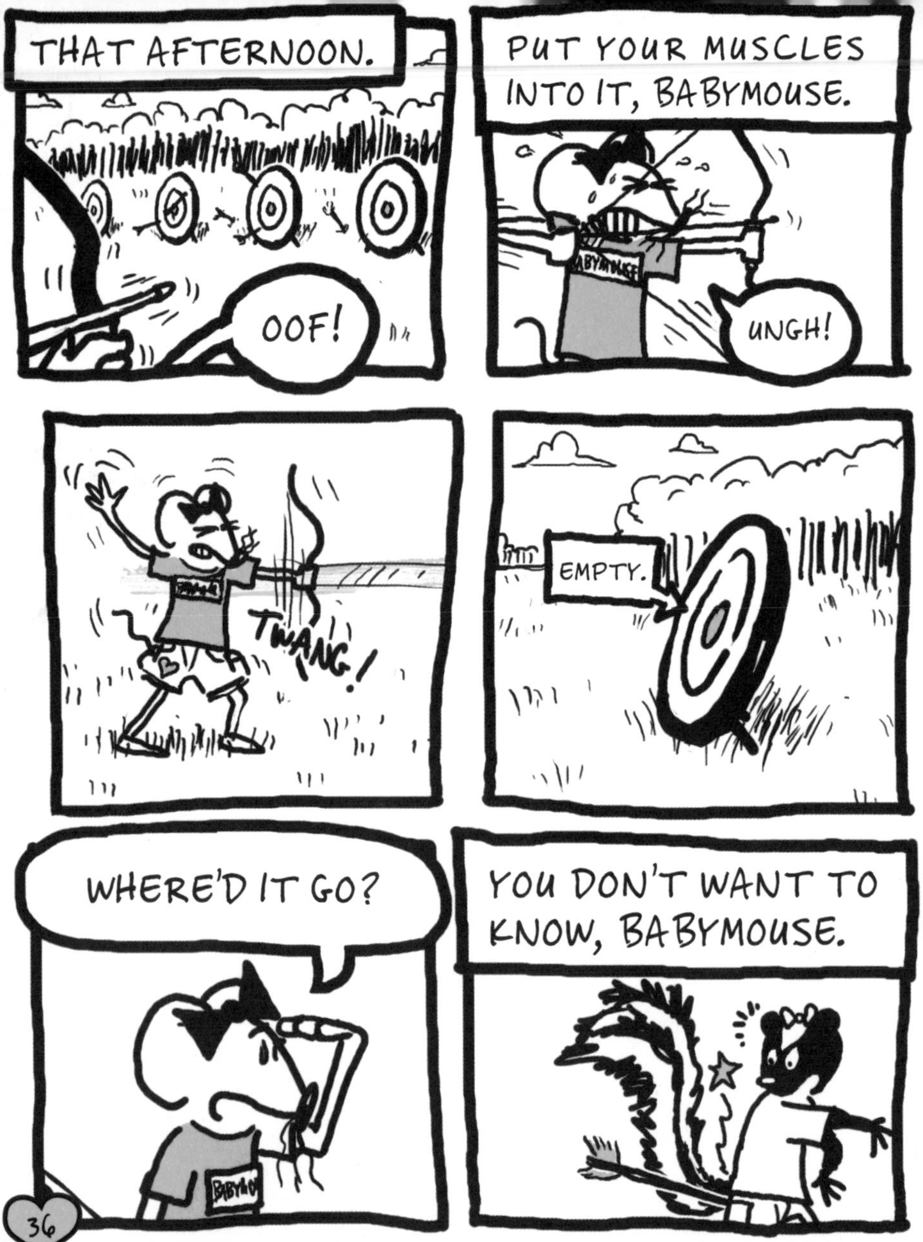
THAT AFTERNOON.
OOF!
PUT YOUR MUSCLES INTO IT, BABYMOUSE.
UNGH!
TWANG!
EMPTY.
WHERE'D IT GO?
YOU DON'T WANT TO KNOW, BABYMOUSE.

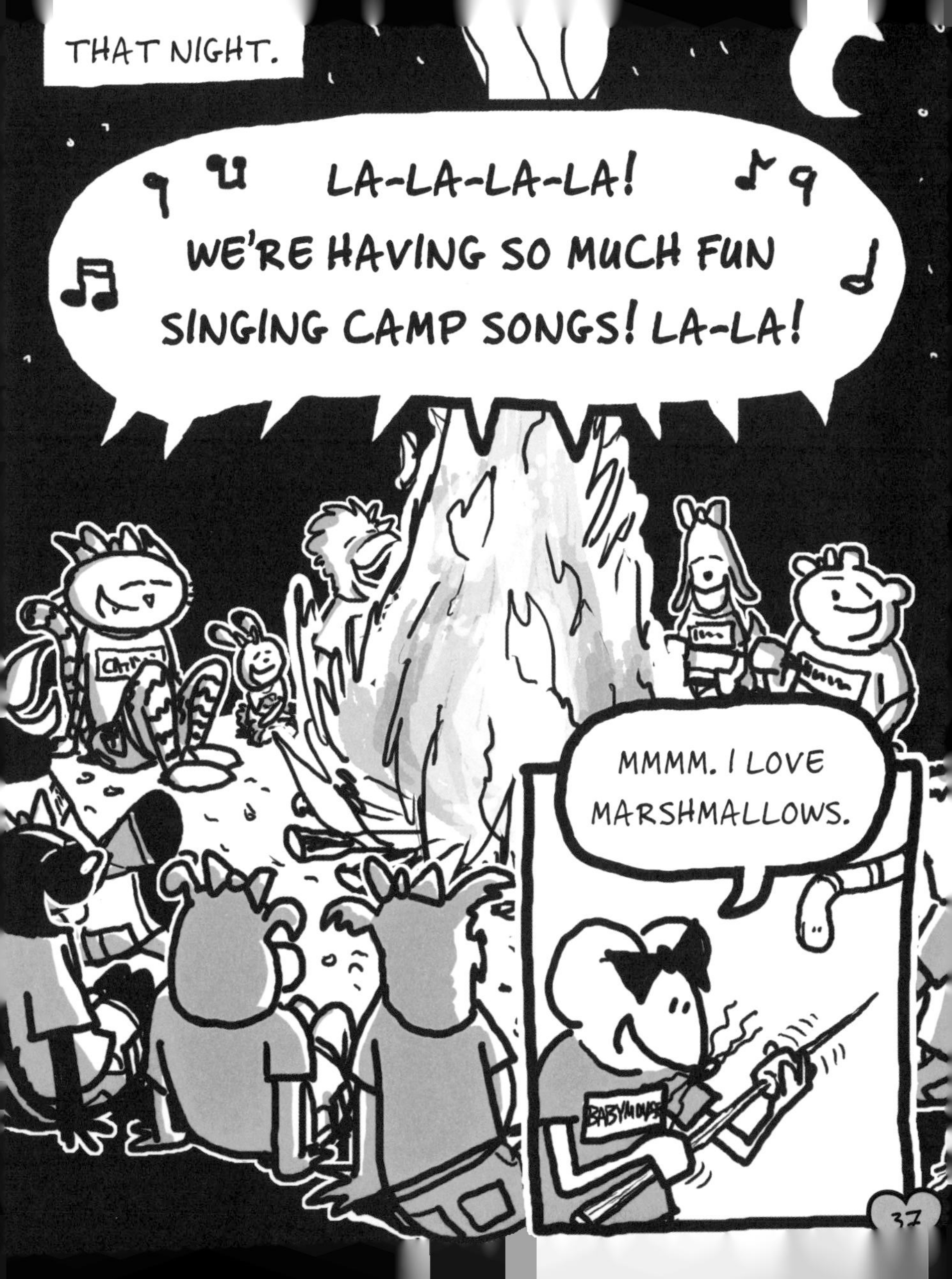
THAT NIGHT.
LA-LA-LA-LA! WE'RE HAVING SO MUCH FUN SINGING CAMP SONGS! LA-LA!
MMMM. I LOVE MARSHMALLOWS.
BABYMOUSE

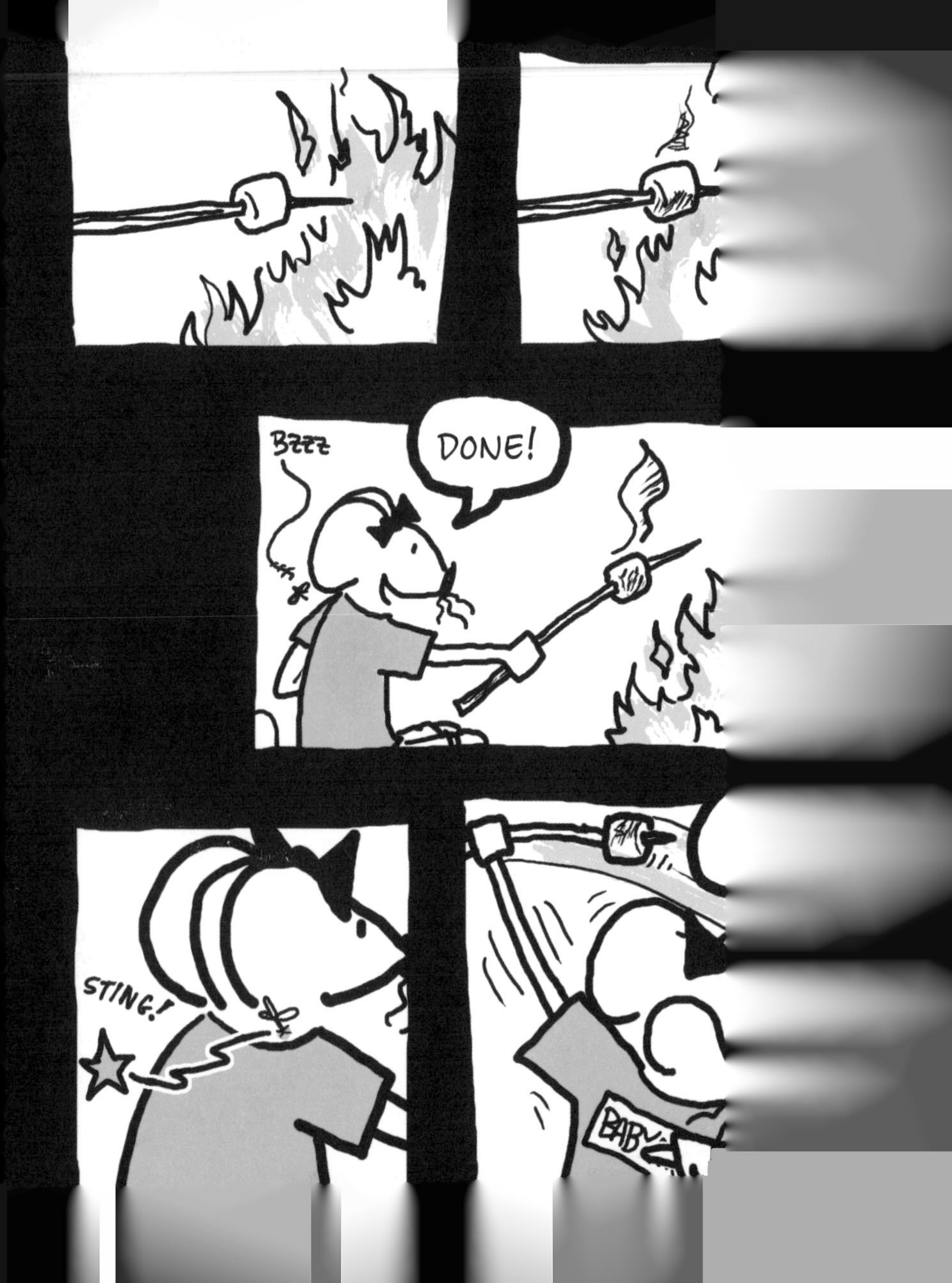
BZZZ
DONE!
STING!
BABY

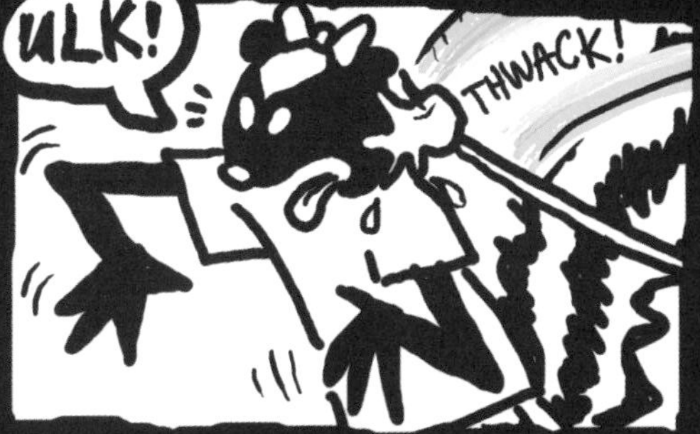
ULK!
THWACK!
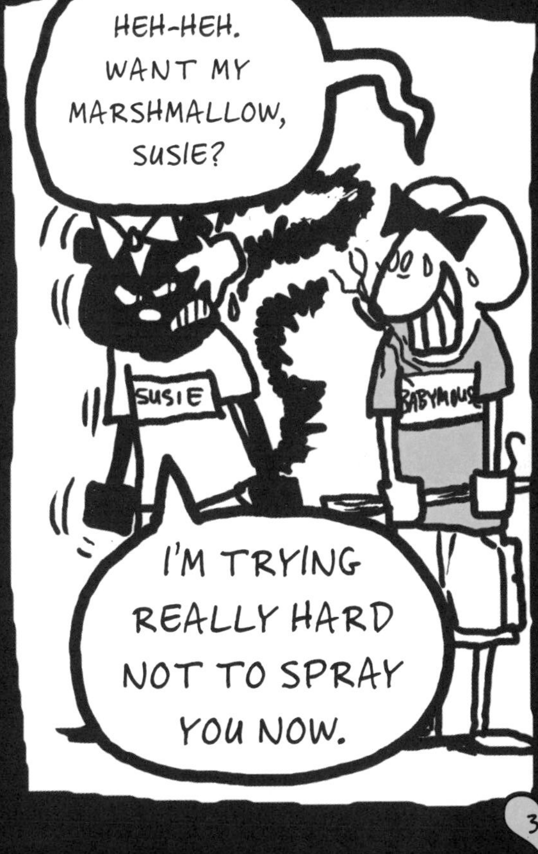
HEH-HEH. WANT MY MARSHMALLOW, SUSIE?
SUSIE
BABYMOUSE
I'M TRYING REALLY HARD NOT TO SPRAY YOU NOW.

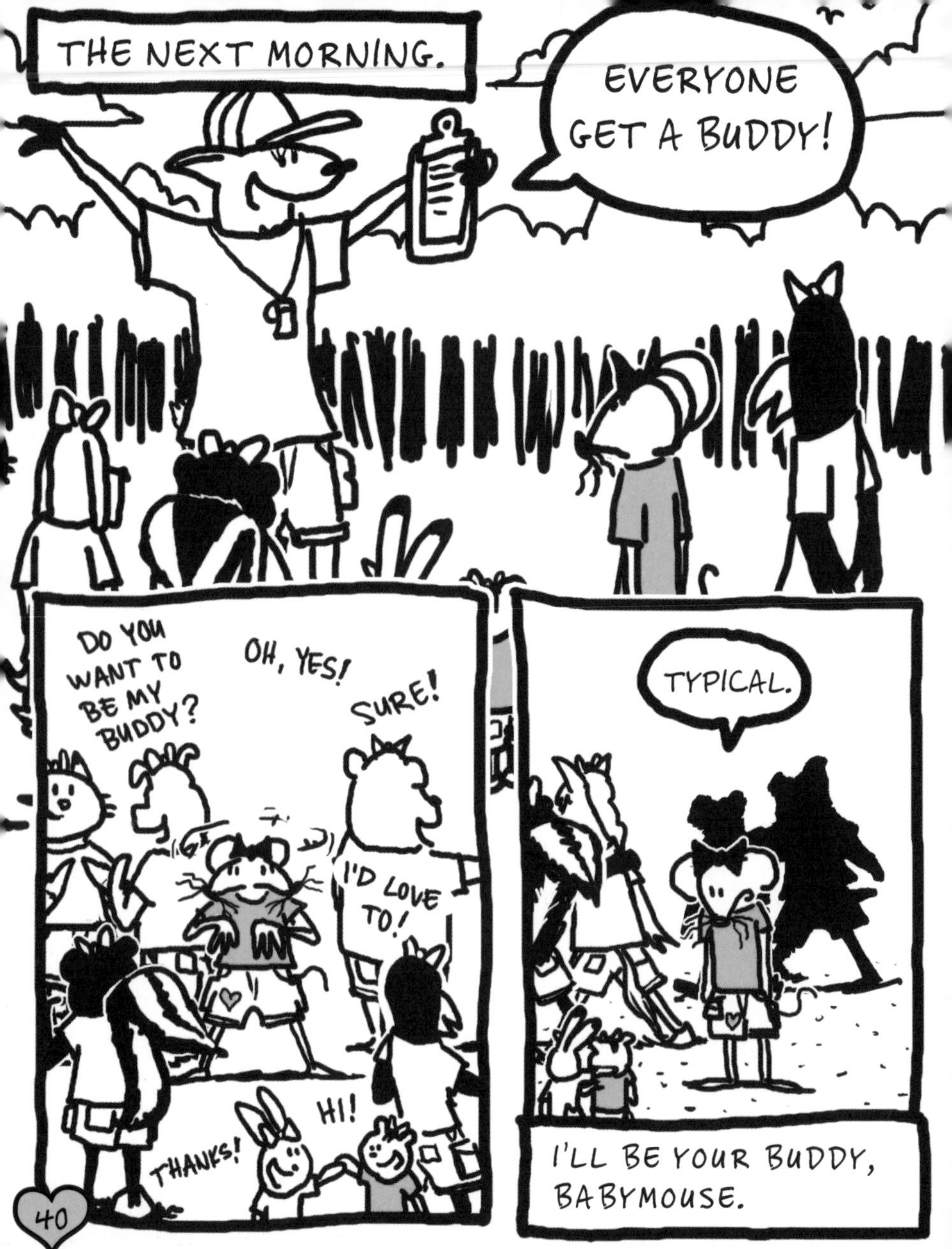
THE NEXT MORNING.
EVERYONE GET A BUDDY!
DO YOU WANT TO BE MY BUDDY?
OH, YES!
SURE!
I'D LOVE TO!
THANKS!
HI!
TYPICAL.
I'LL BE YOUR BUDDY, BABYMOUSE.

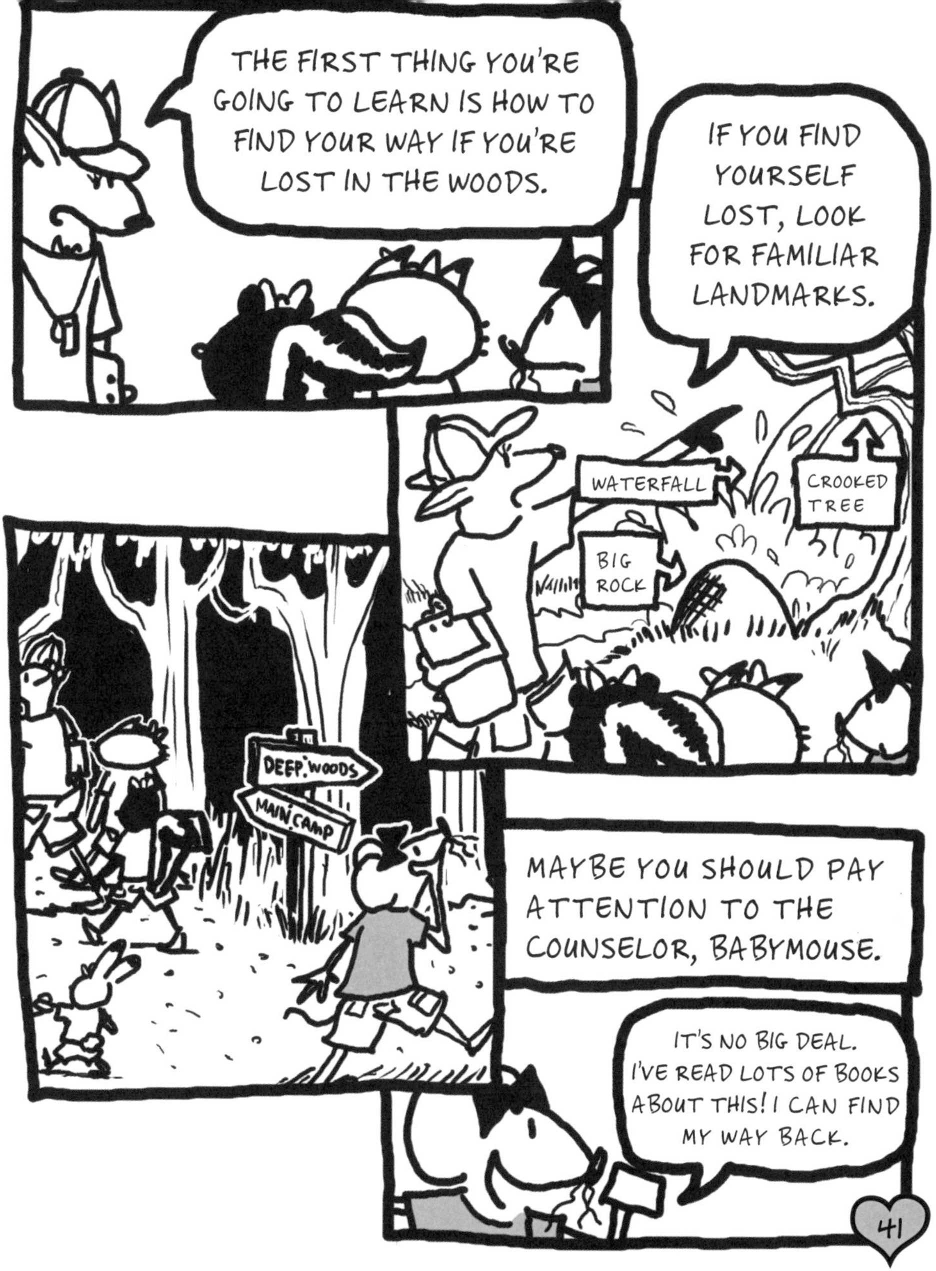
THE FIRST THING YOU'RE GOING TO LEARN IS HOW TO FIND YOUR WAY IF YOU'RE LOST IN THE WOODS.
IF YOU FIND YOURSELF LOST, LOOK FOR FAMILIAR LANDMARKS.
WATERFALL
CROOKED TREE
BIG ROCK
DEEP WOODS
MAIN CAMP
MAYBE YOU SHOULD PAY ATTENTION TO THE COUNSELOR, BABYMOUSE.
IT'S NO BIG DEAL. I'VE READ LOTS OF BOOKS ABOUT THIS! I CAN FIND MY WAY BACK.

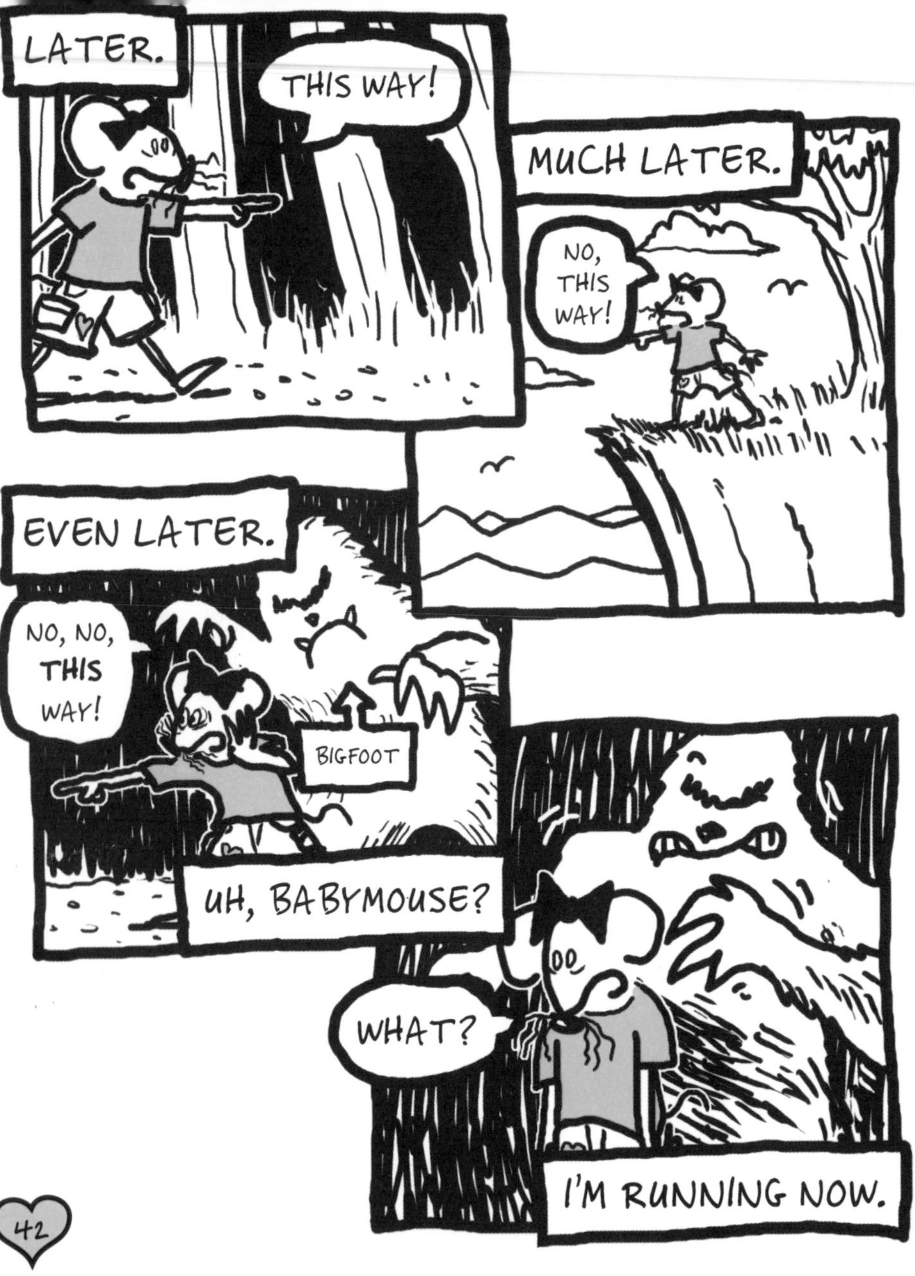
LATER.
THIS WAY!
MUCH LATER.
NO, THIS WAY!
EVEN LATER.
NO, NO, THIS WAY!
BIGFOOT
UH, BABYMOUSE?
WHAT?
I'M RUNNING NOW.

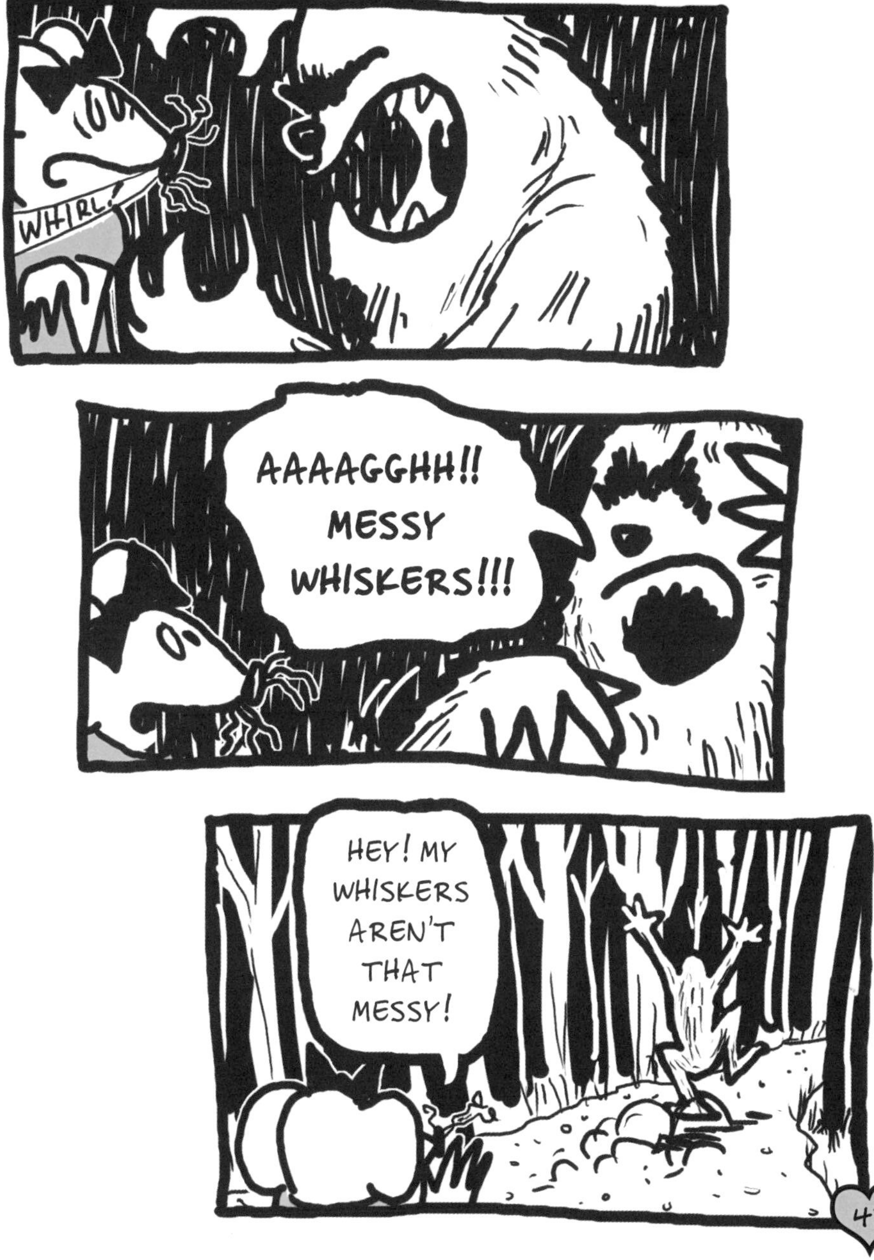
WHIRL!
AAAAGGHH!! MESSY WHISKERS!!!
HEY! MY WHISKERS AREN'T THAT MESSY!

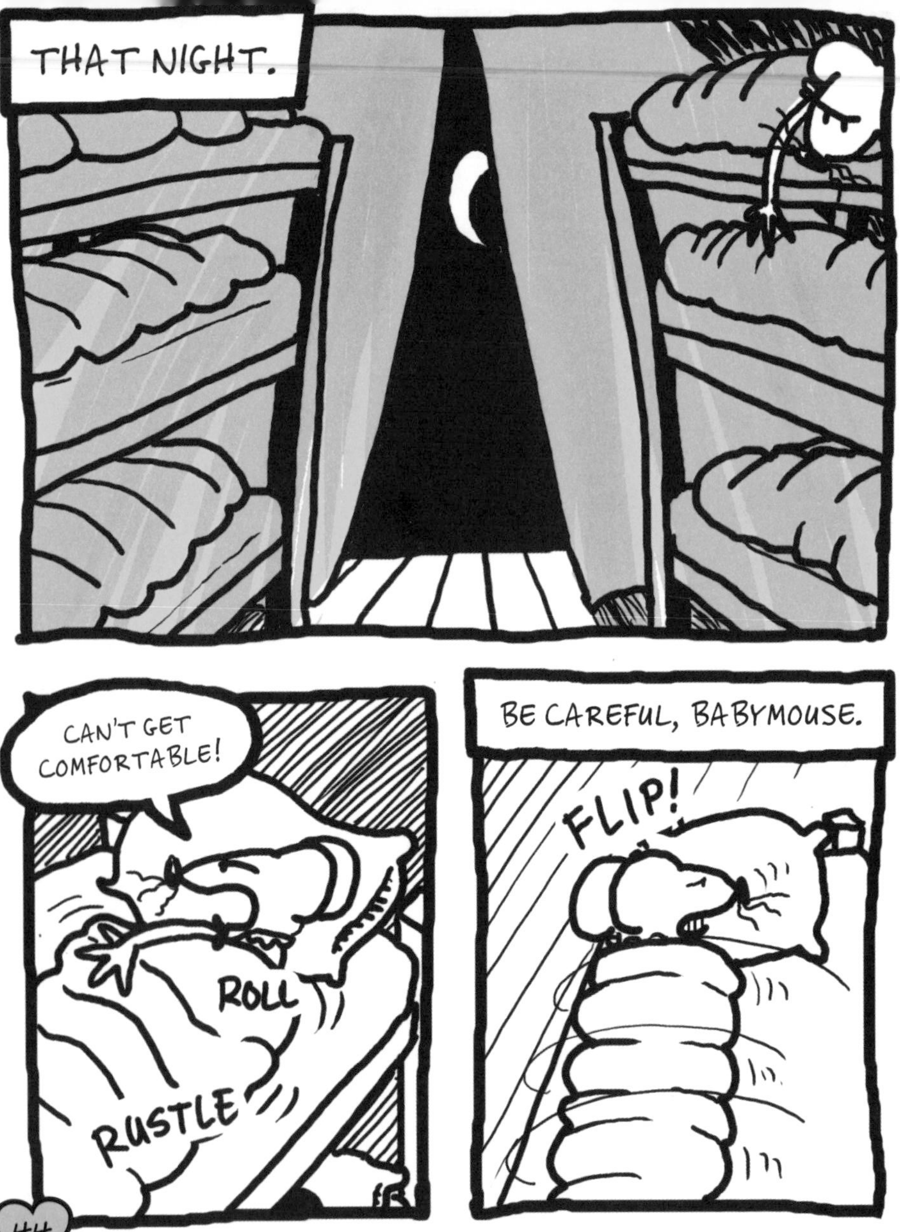
THAT NIGHT.
CAN'T GET COMFORTABLE!
ROLL
RUSTLE
BE CAREFUL, BABYMOUSE.
FLIP!

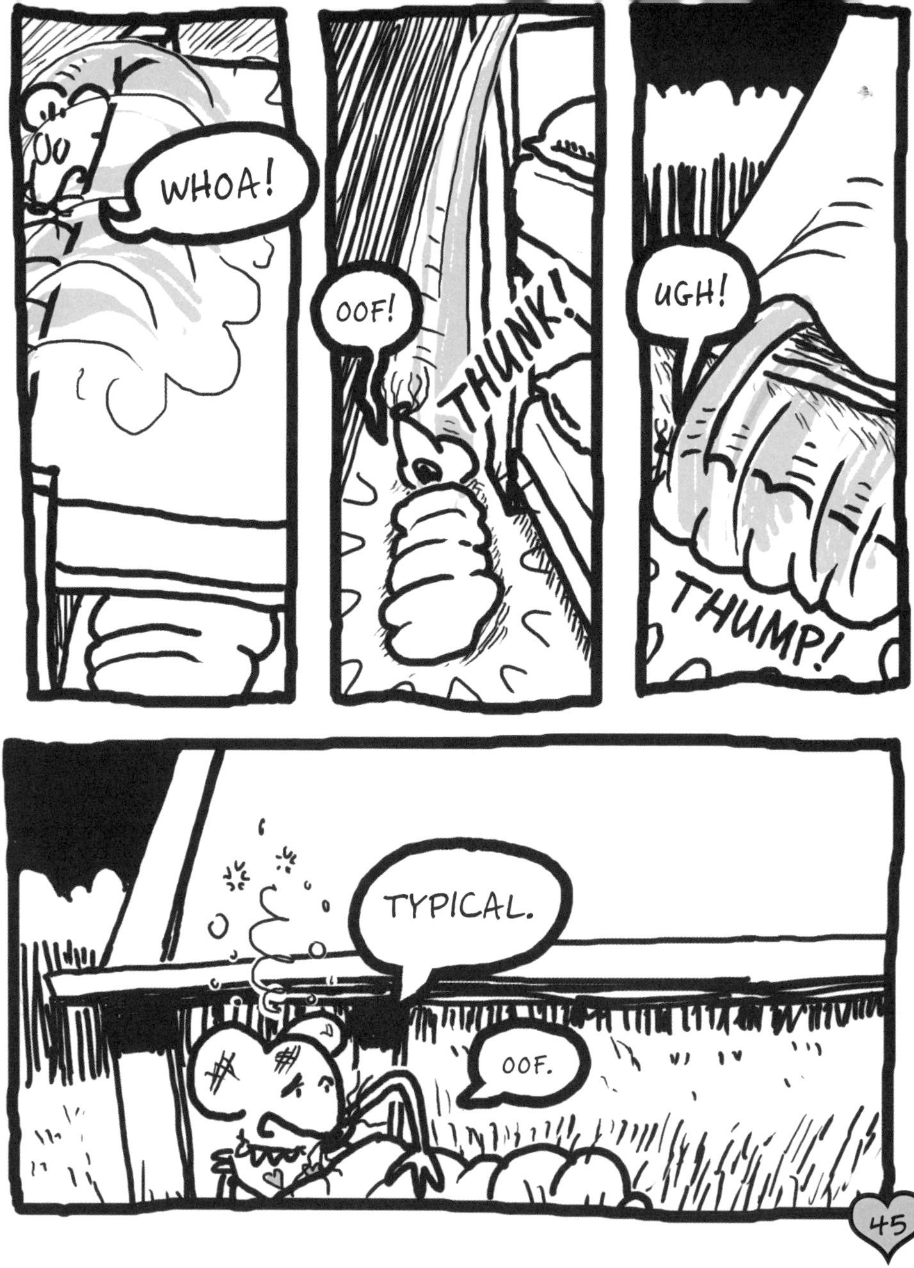
WHOA!
OOF!
THUNK!
UGH!
THUMP!
TYPICAL.
OOF.

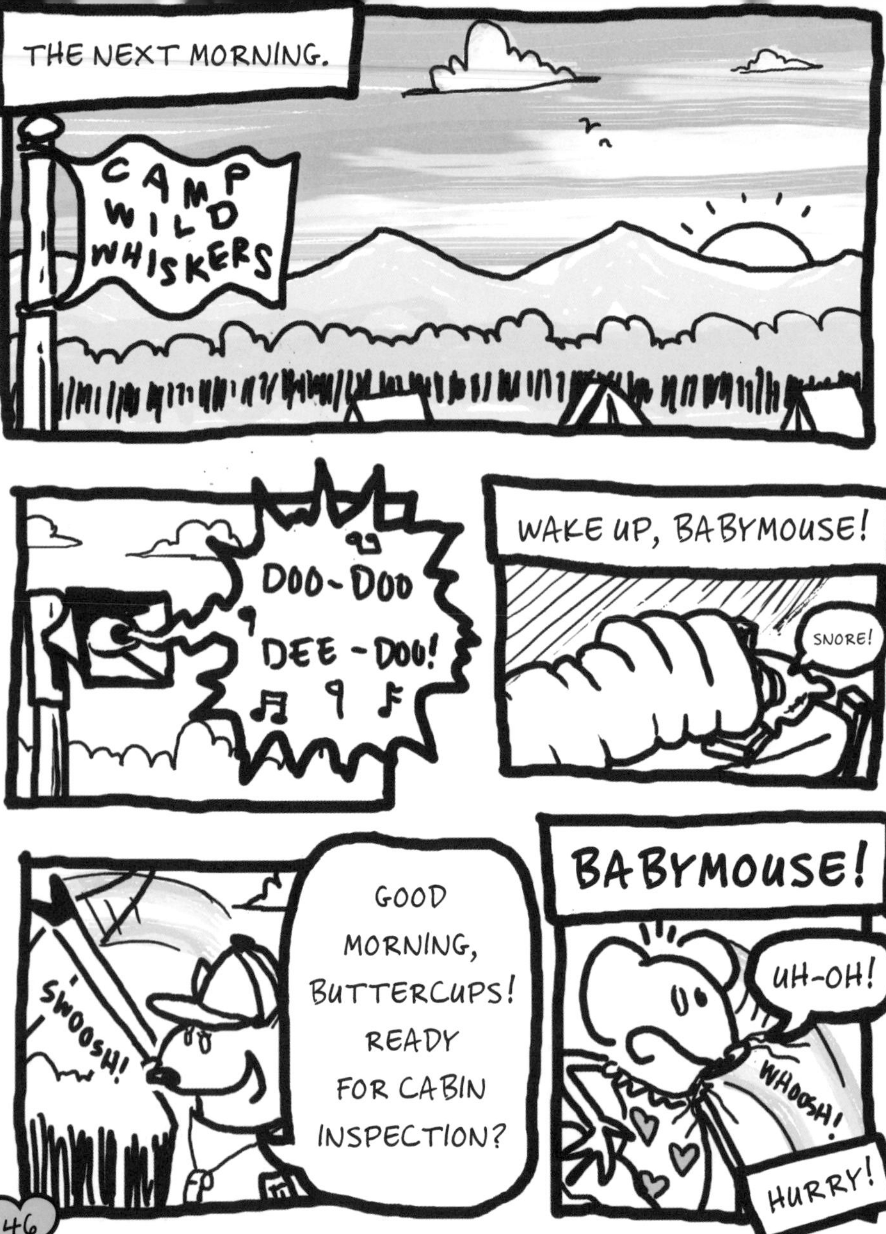
THE NEXT MORNING.
CAMP WILD WHISKERS
DOO-DOO DEE-DOO!
WAKE UP, BABYMOUSE!
SNORE!
SWOOSH!
GOOD MORNING, BUTTERCUPS! READY FOR CABIN INSPECTION?
BABYMOUSE!
UH-OH!
WHOOSH!
HURRY!

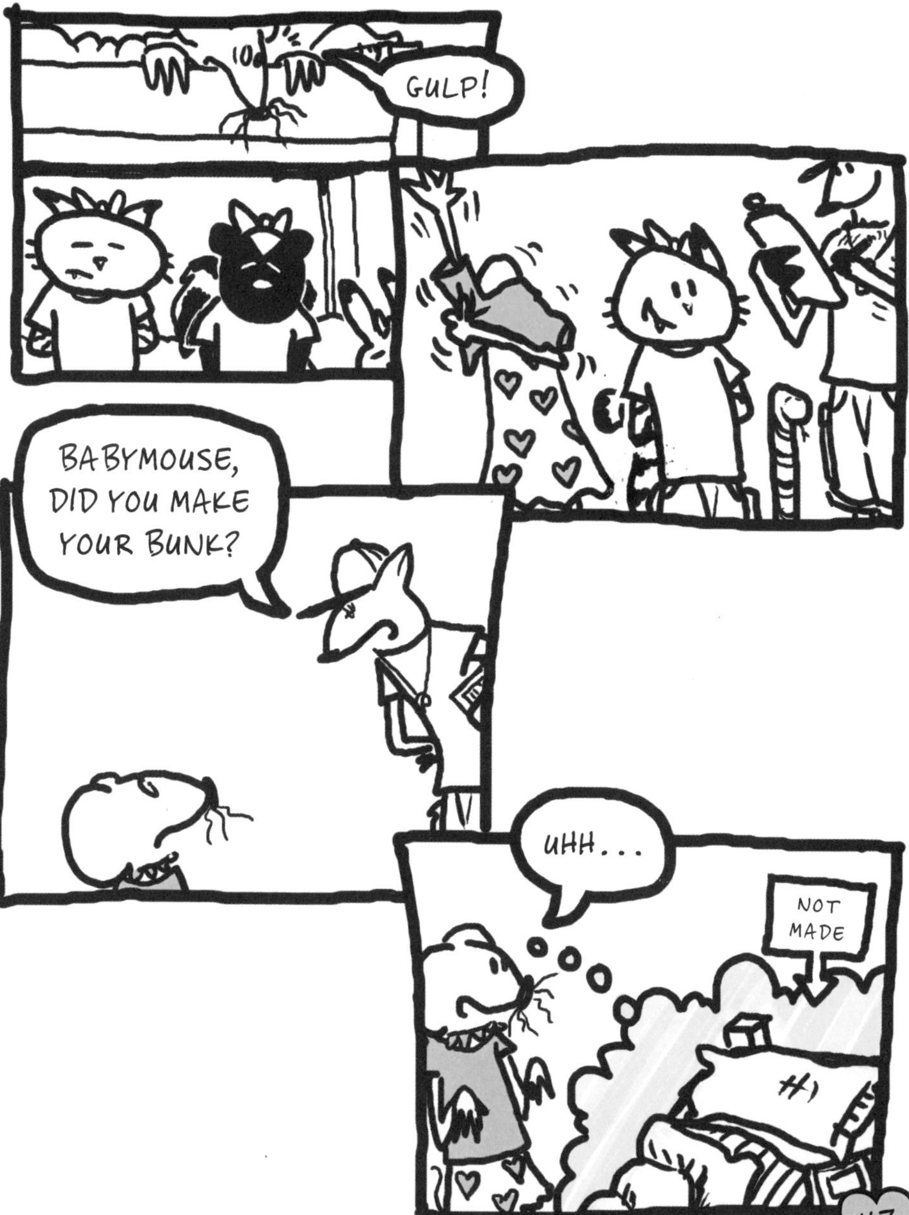
GULP!
BABYMOUSE, DID YOU MAKE YOUR BUNK?
UHH...
NOT MADE

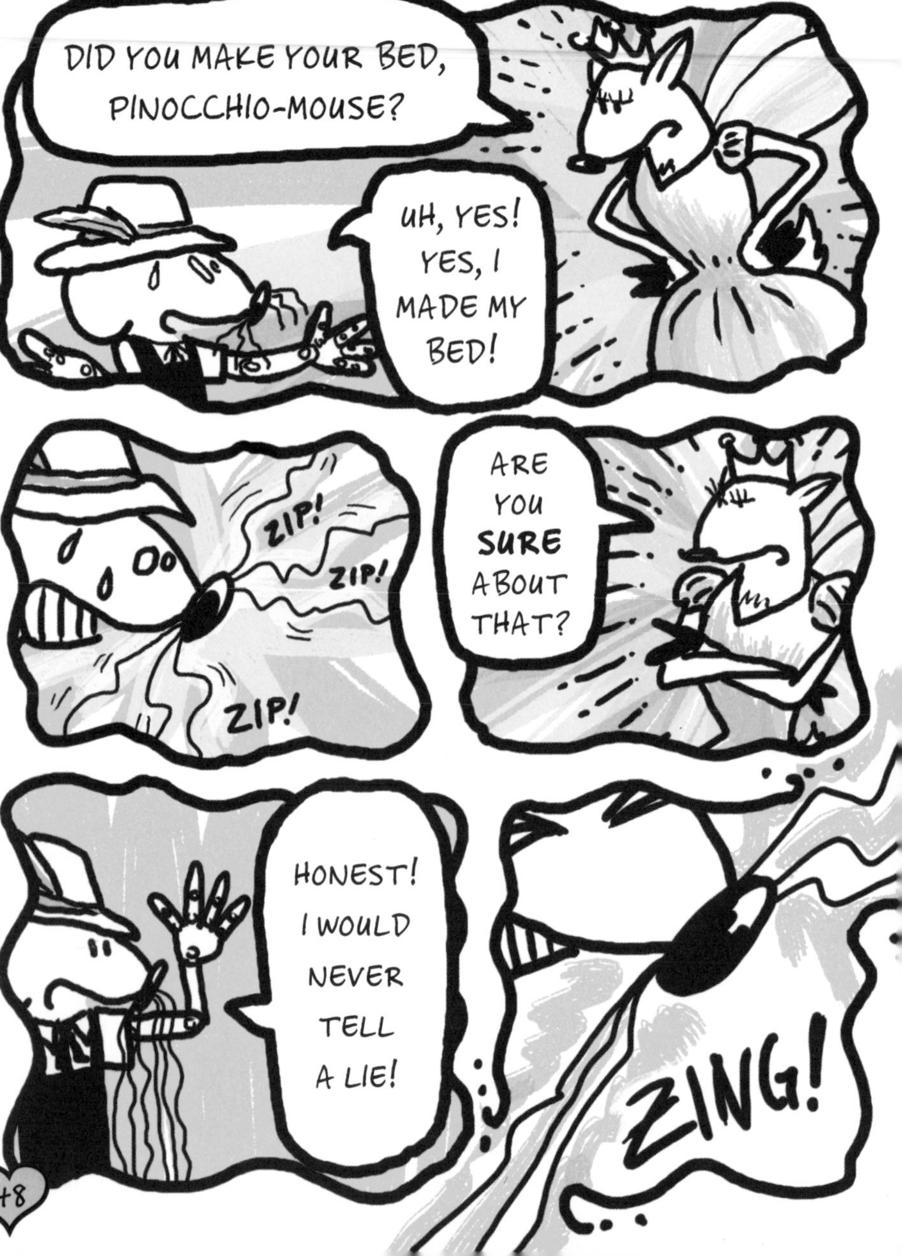
DID YOU MAKE YOUR BED, PINOCCHIO-MOUSE?
UH, YES! YES, I MADE MY BED!
ZIP!
ZIP!
ZIP!
ARE YOU **SURE** ABOUT THAT?
HONEST! I WOULD NEVER TELL A LIE!
ZING!

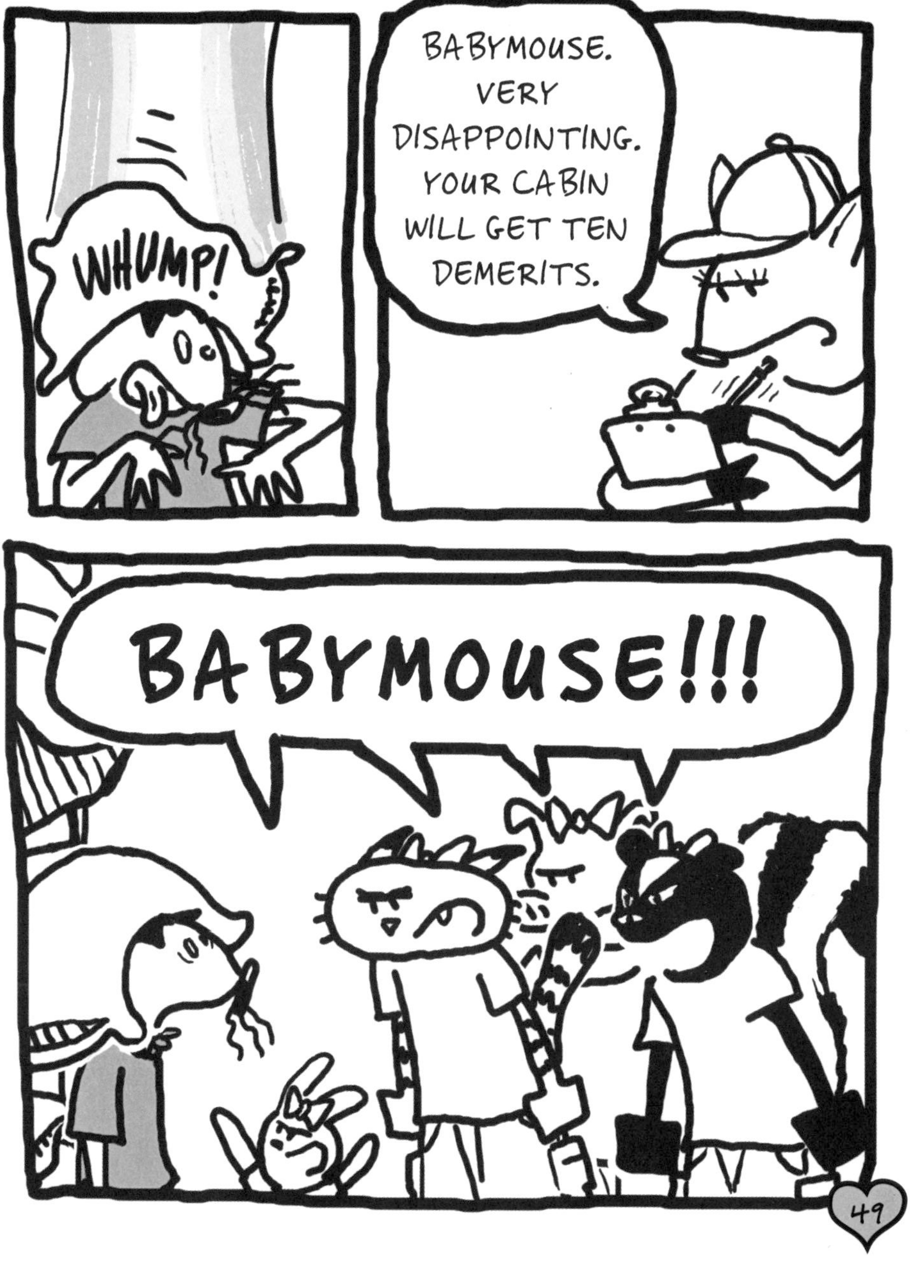

WHUMP!
BABYMOUSE. VERY DISAPPOINTING. YOUR CABIN WILL GET TEN DEMERITS.
BABYMOUSE!!!

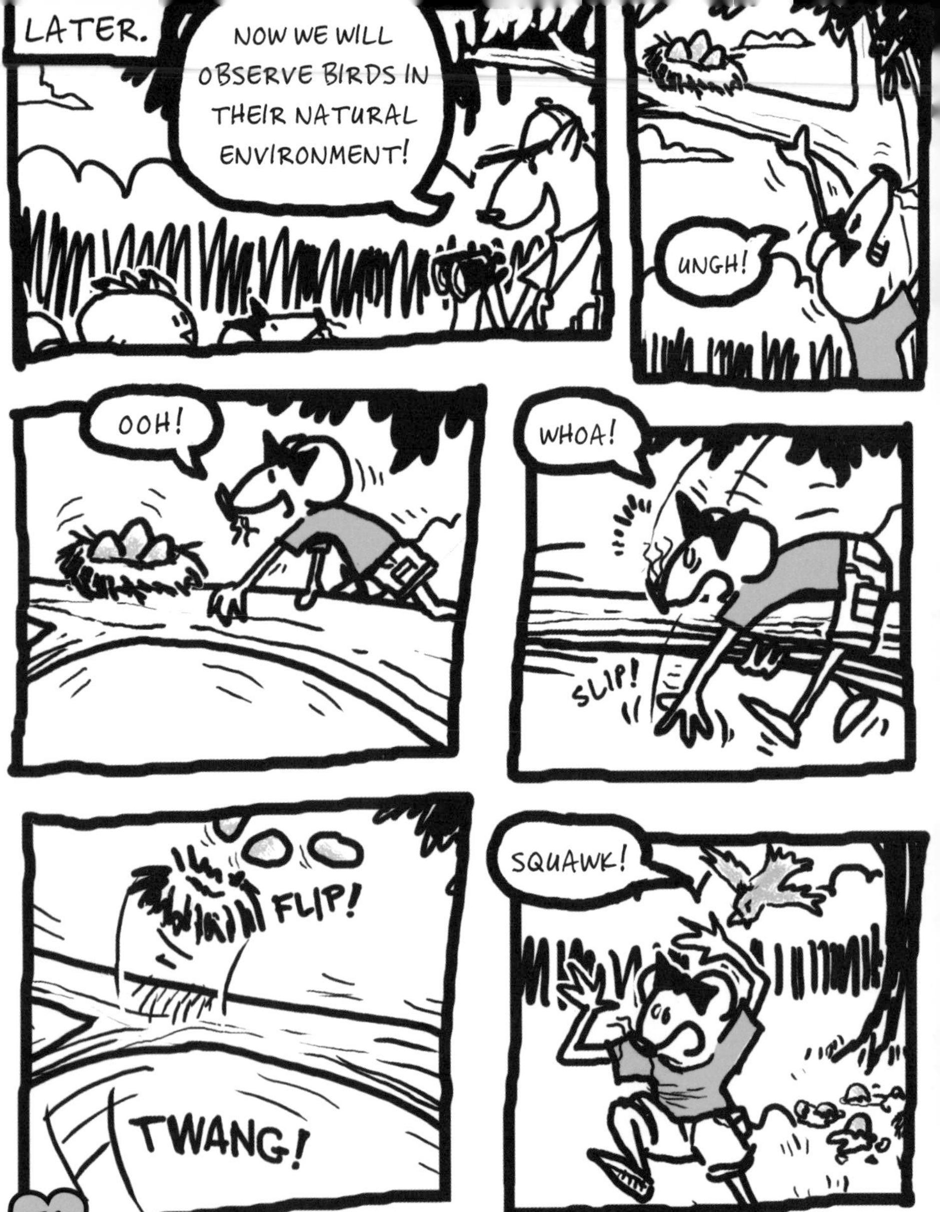
LATER.
NOW WE WILL OBSERVE BIRDS IN THEIR NATURAL ENVIRONMENT!
UNGH!
OOH!
WHOA!
SLIP!
FLIP!
TWANG!
SQUAWK!

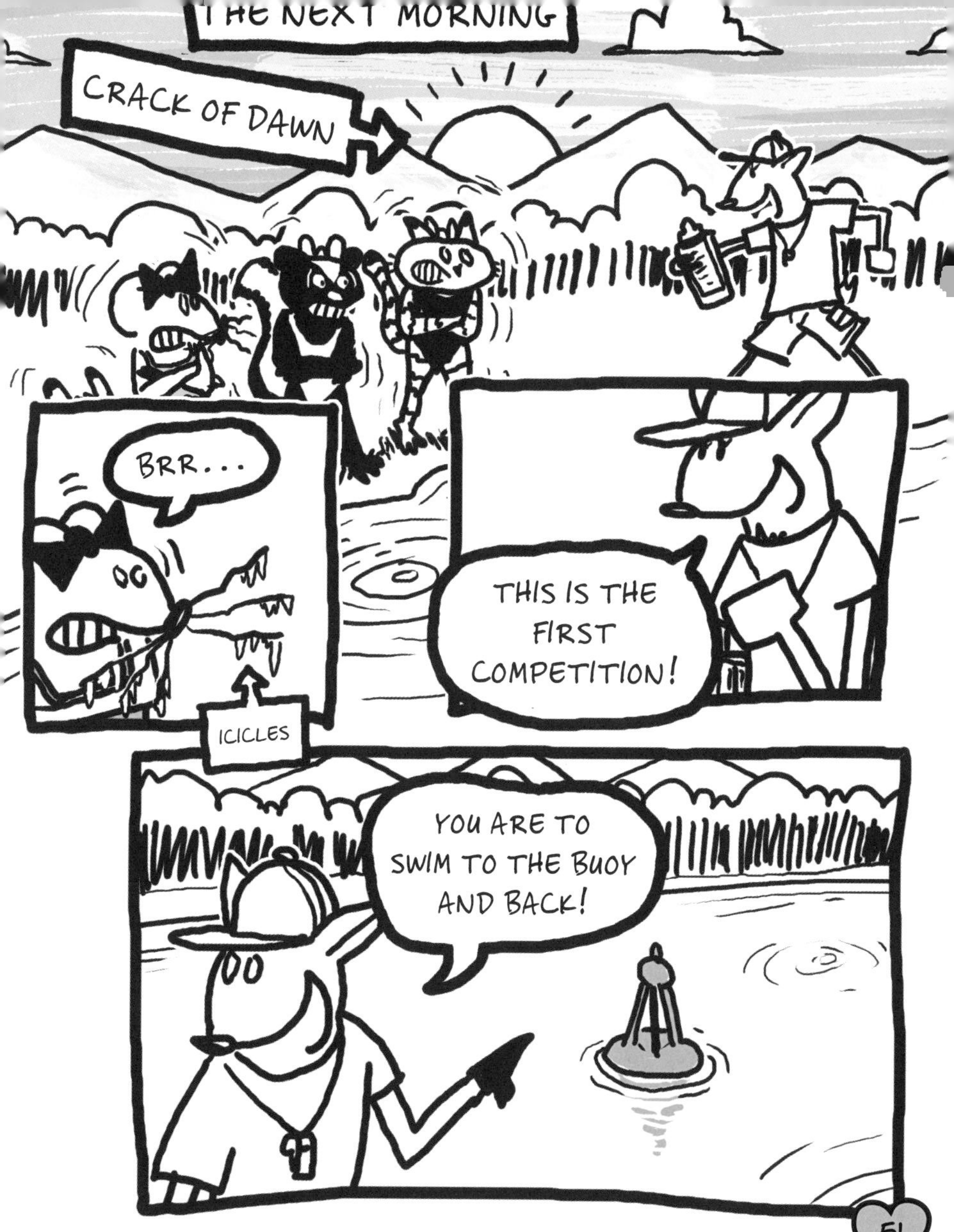
THE NEXT MORNING
CRACK OF DAWN
BRR...
ICICLES
THIS IS THE FIRST COMPETITION!
YOU ARE TO SWIM TO THE BUOY AND BACK!

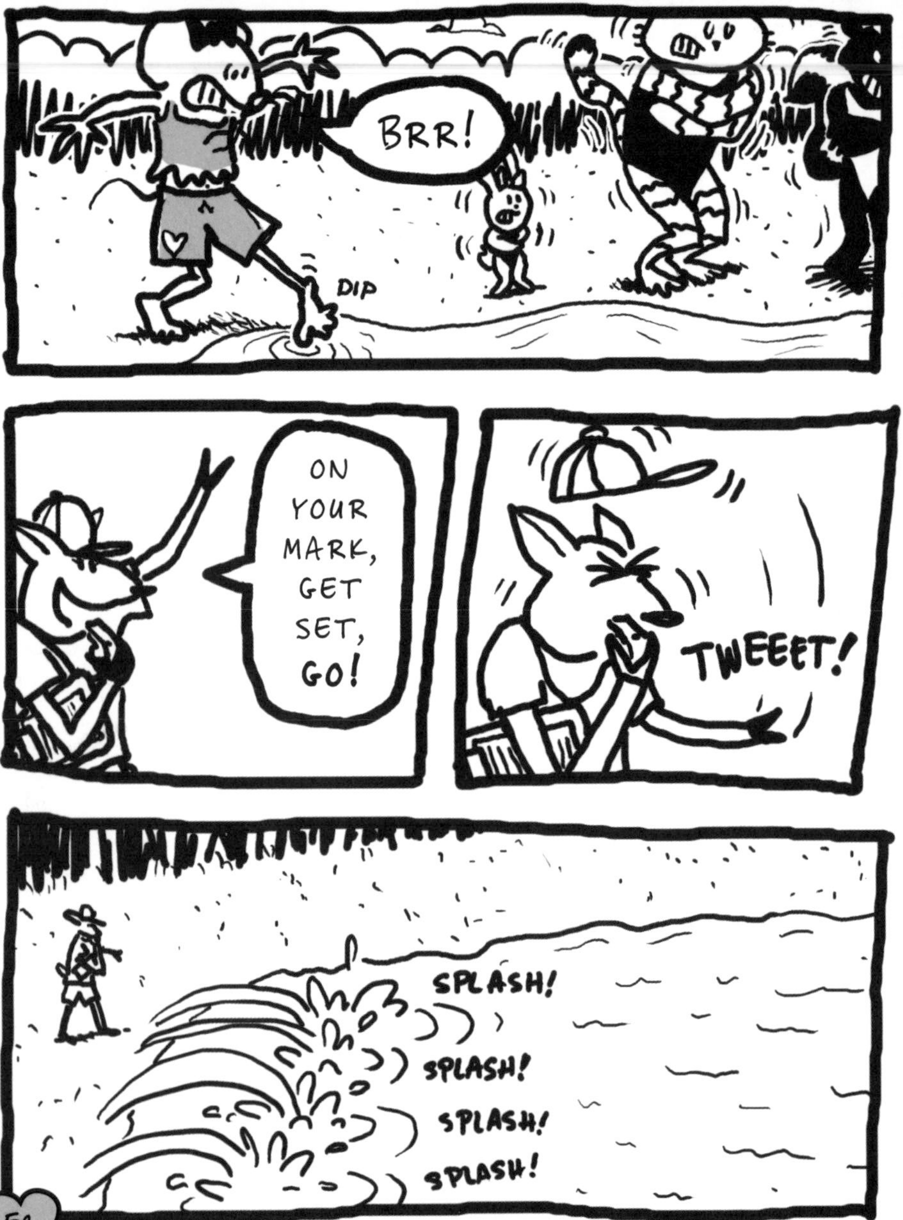
BRR!
DIP
ON YOUR MARK, GET SET, GO!
TWEEET!
SPLASH!
SPLASH!
SPLASH!
SPLASH!

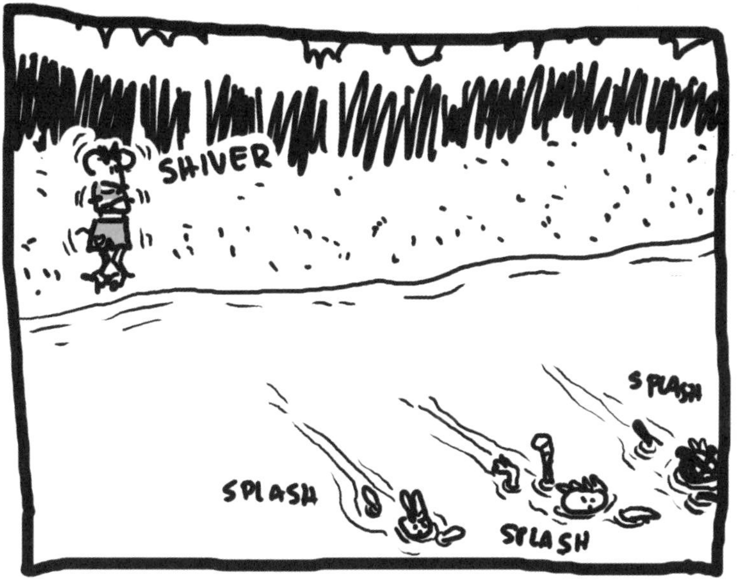
SHIVER
SPLASH
SPLASH
SPLASH
SPLASH

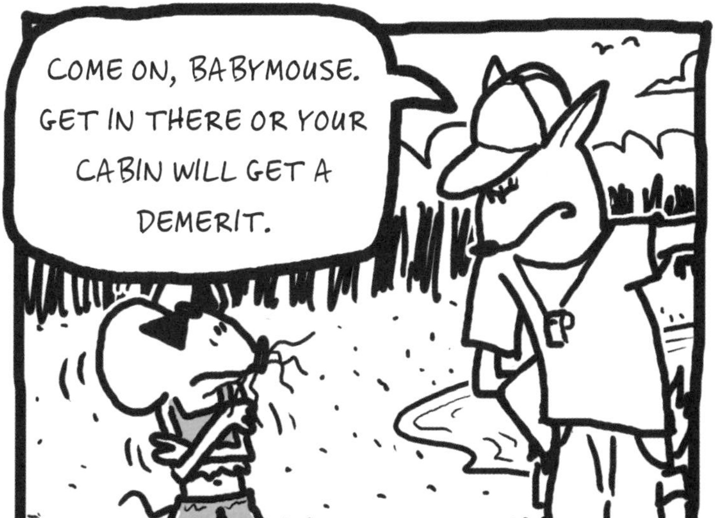
COME ON, BABYMOUSE. GET IN THERE OR YOUR CABIN WILL GET A DEMERIT.

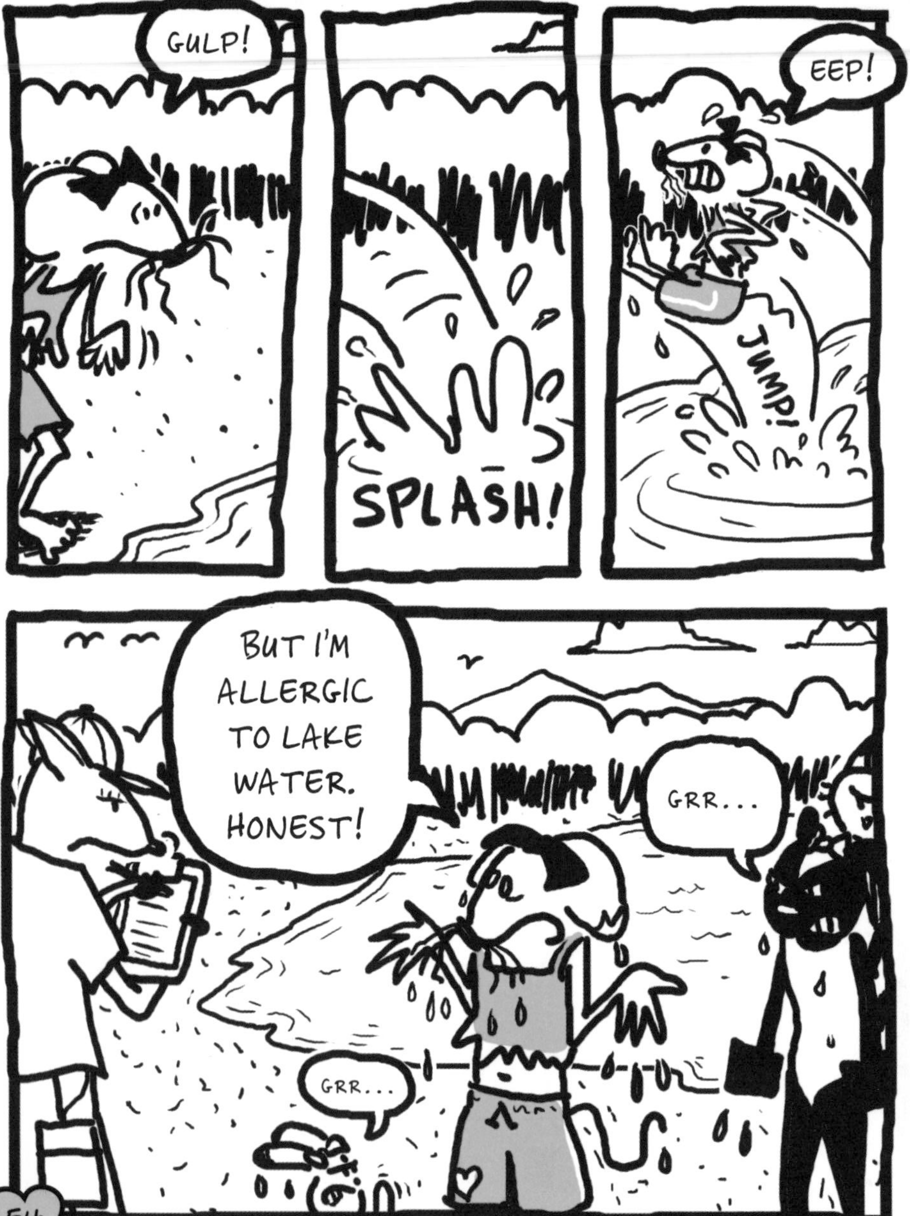
GULP!
SPLASH!
EEP!
JUMP!
BUT I'M ALLERGIC TO LAKE WATER. HONEST!
GRR...
GRR...

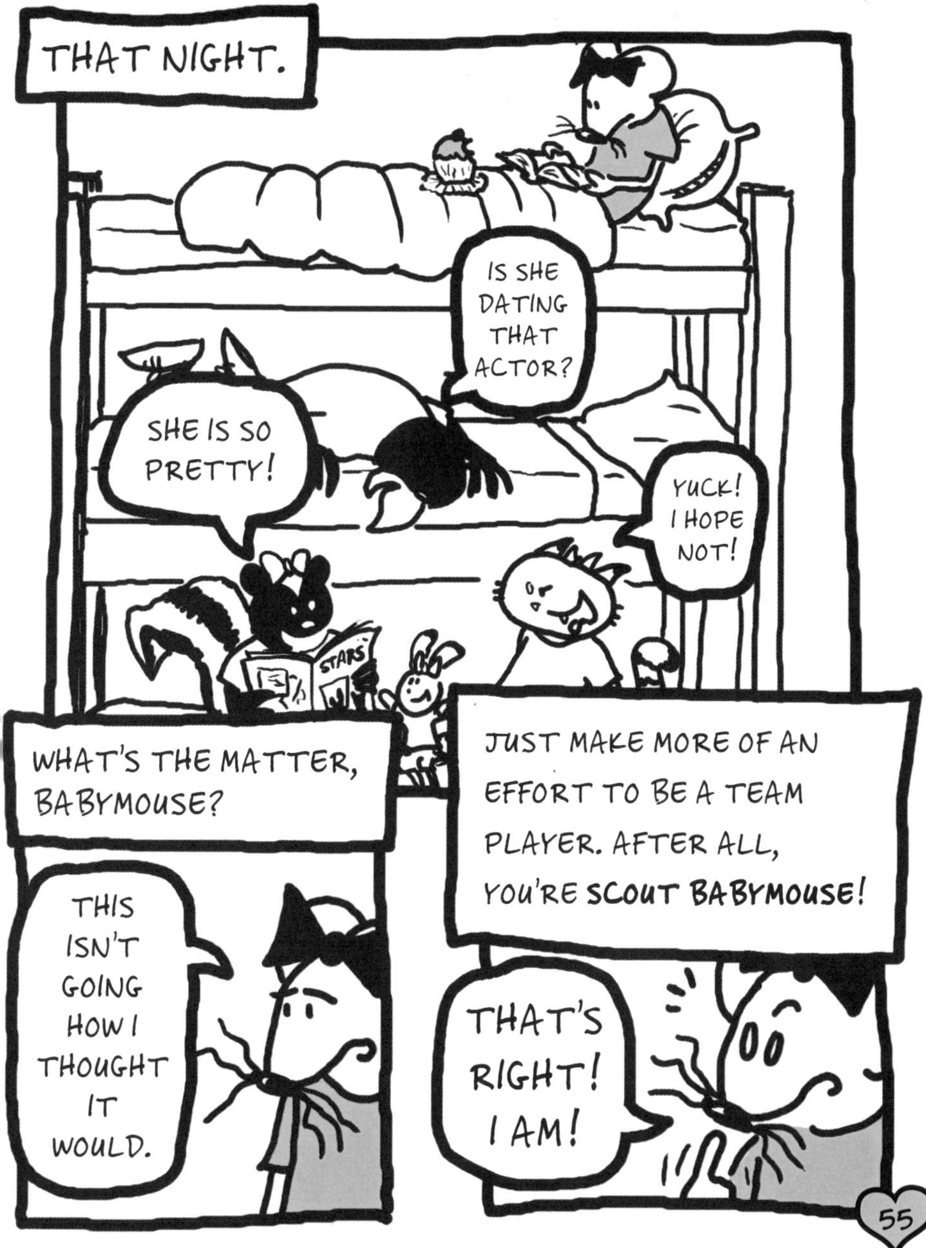
THAT NIGHT.
IS SHE DATING THAT ACTOR?
SHE IS SO PRETTY!
YUCK! I HOPE NOT!
STARS
WHAT'S THE MATTER, BABYMOUSE?
THIS ISN'T GOING HOW I THOUGHT IT WOULD.
JUST MAKE MORE OF AN EFFORT TO BE A TEAM PLAYER. AFTER ALL, YOU'RE **SCOUT BABYMOUSE**!
THAT'S RIGHT! I AM!

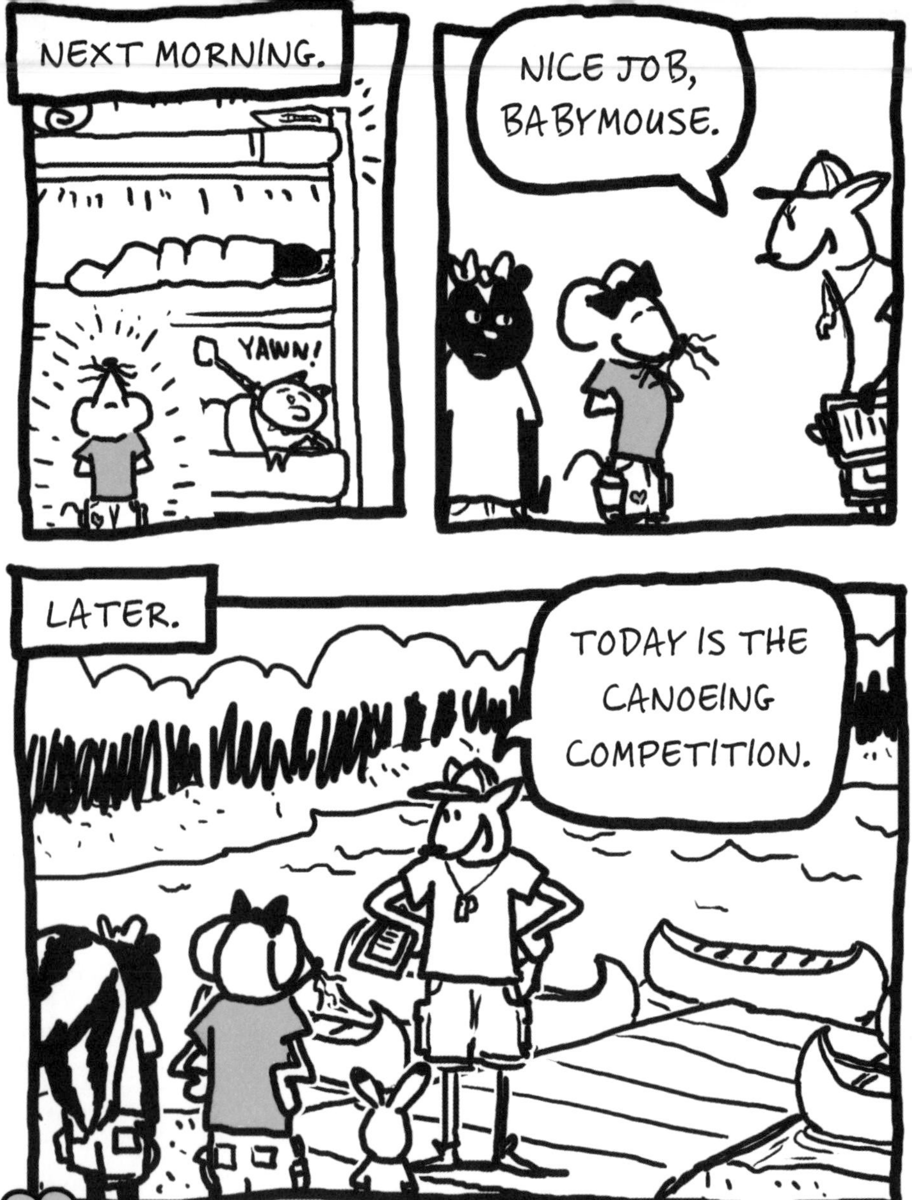
NEXT MORNING.
YAWN!
NICE JOB, BABYMOUSE.
LATER.
TODAY IS THE CANOEING COMPETITION.

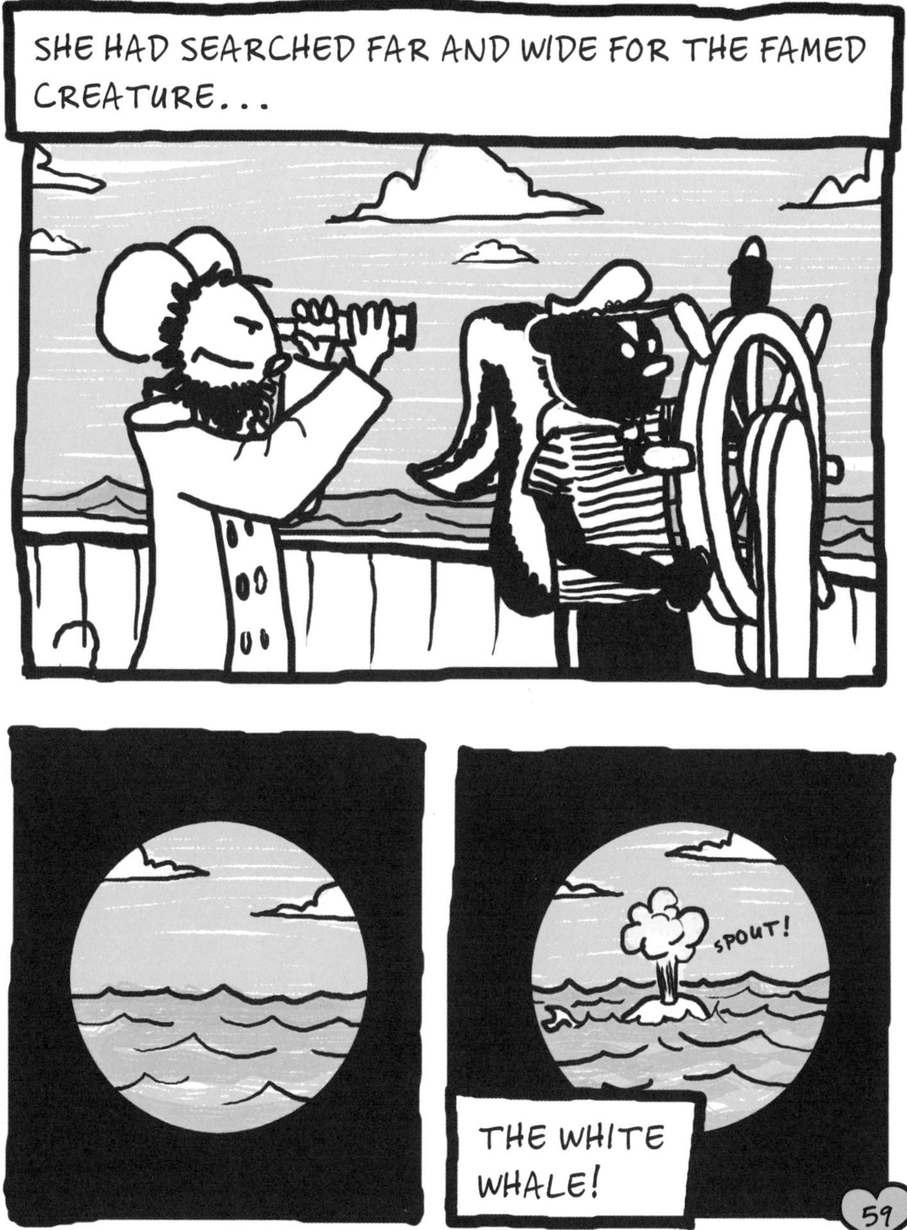
SHE HAD SEARCHED FAR AND WIDE FOR THE FAMED CREATURE...
SPOUT!
THE WHITE WHALE!

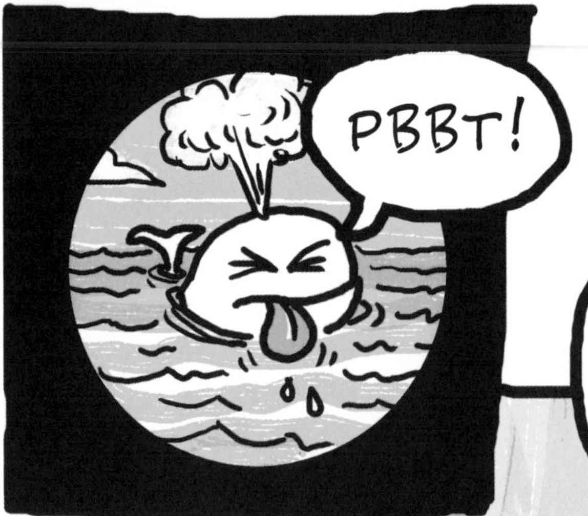
PBBT!

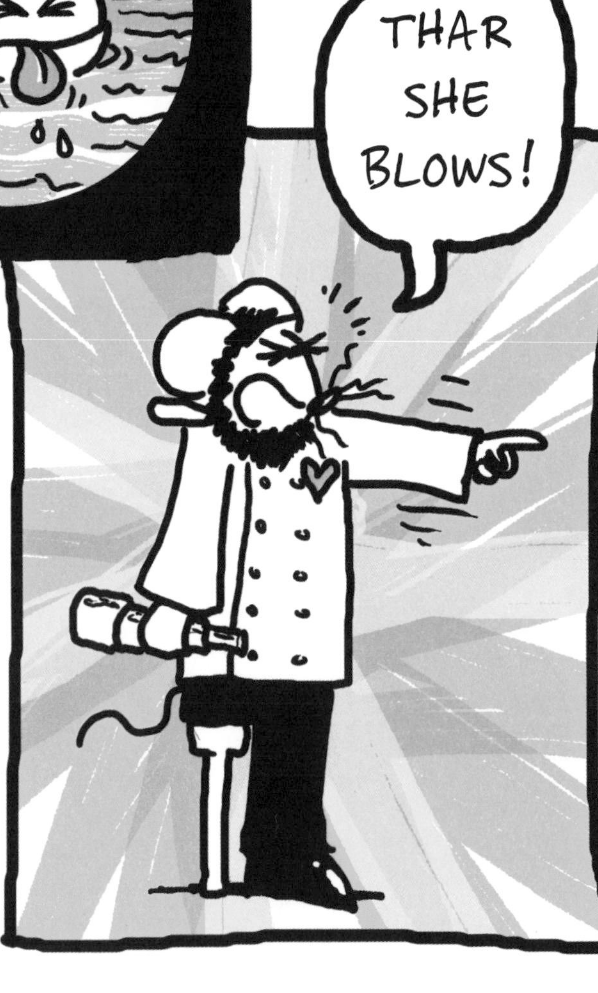
THAR SHE BLOWS!

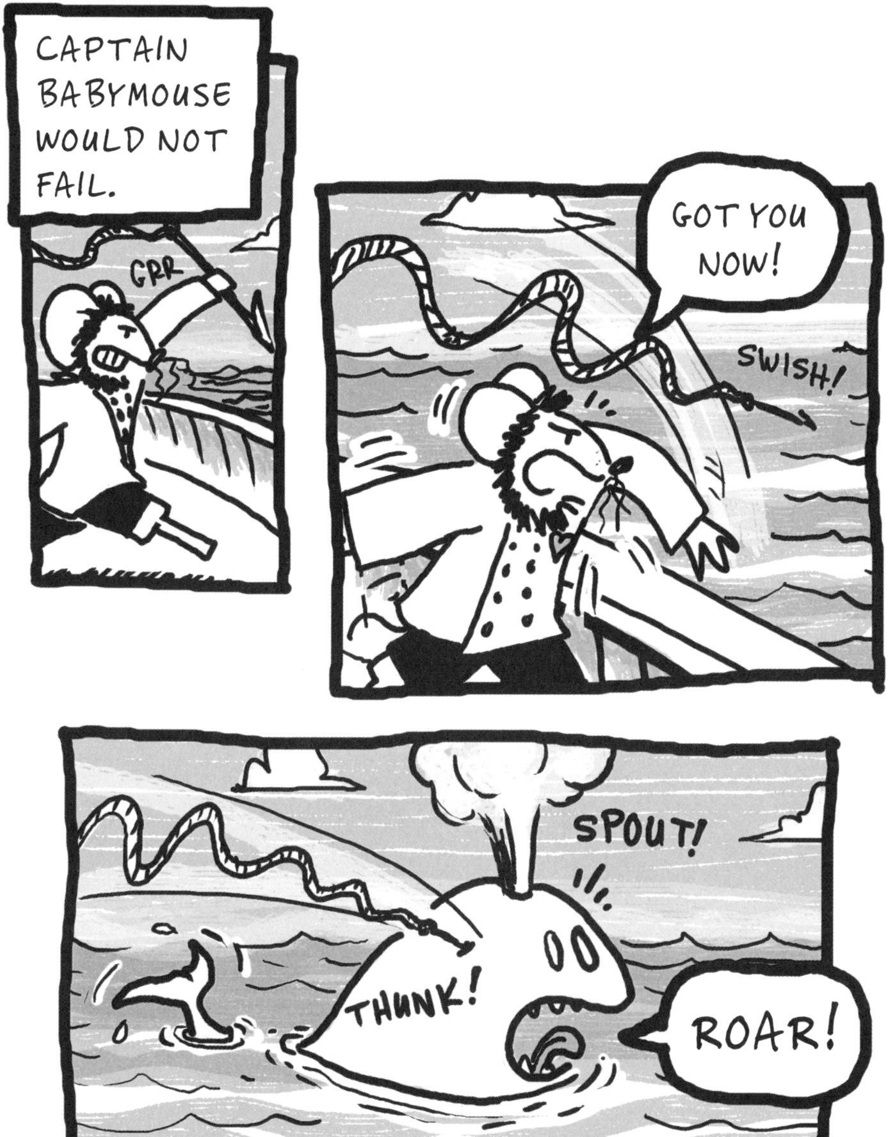
CAPTAIN BABYMOUSE WOULD NOT FAIL.
GRR
GOT YOU NOW!
SWISH!
SPOUT!
THUNK!
ROAR!

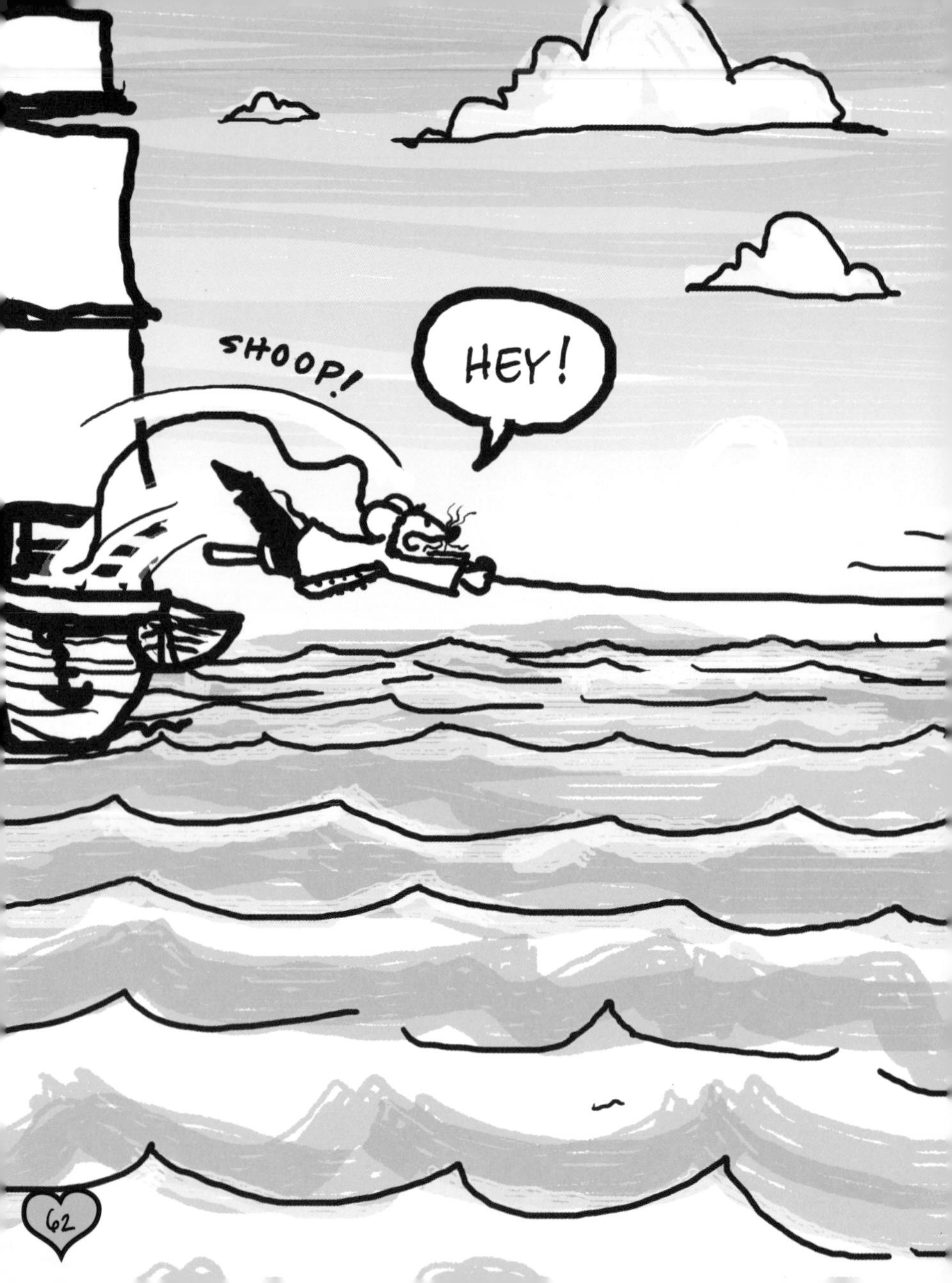
SHOOP!
HEY!

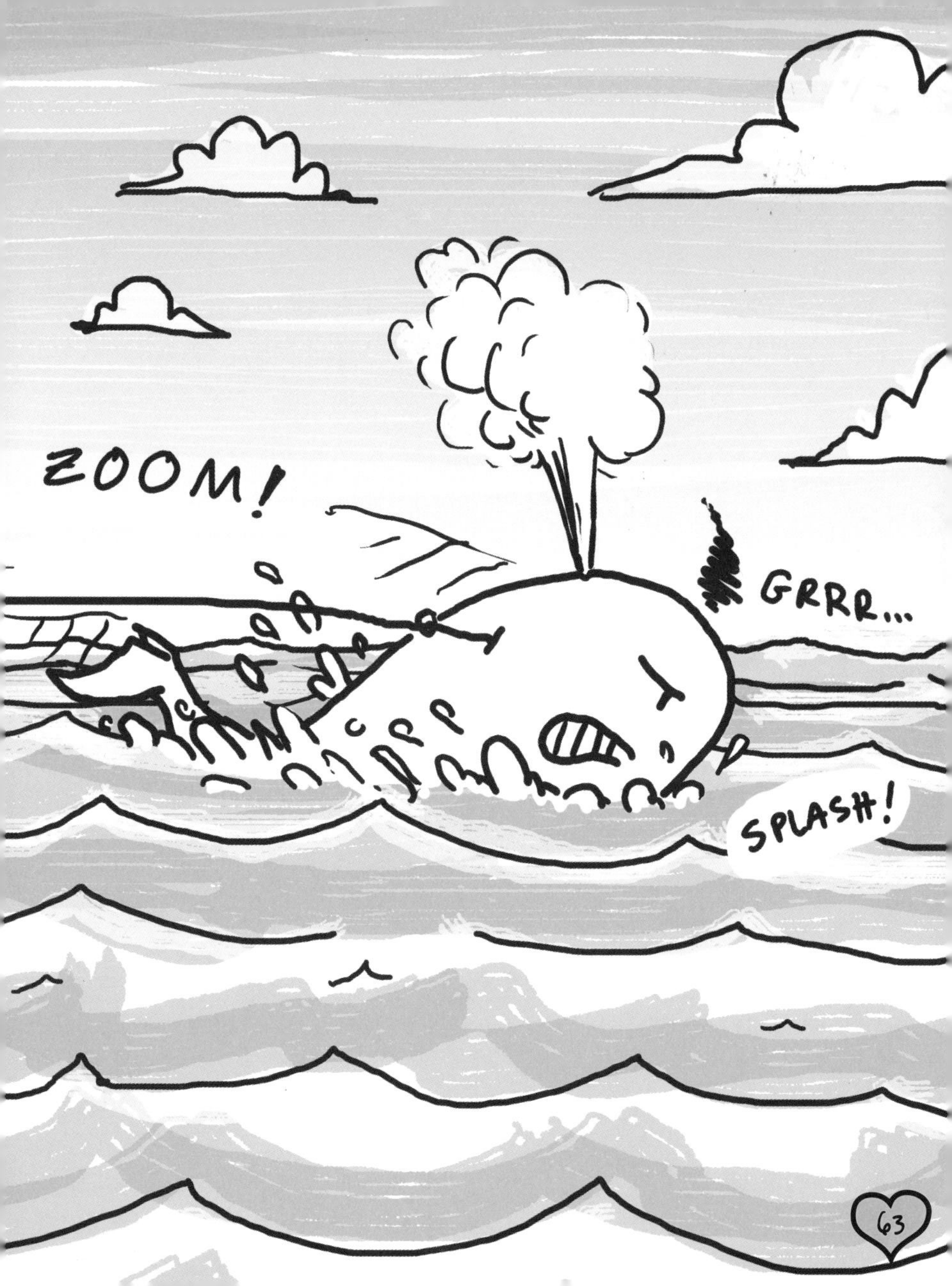
ZOOM!
GRRR...
SPLASH!

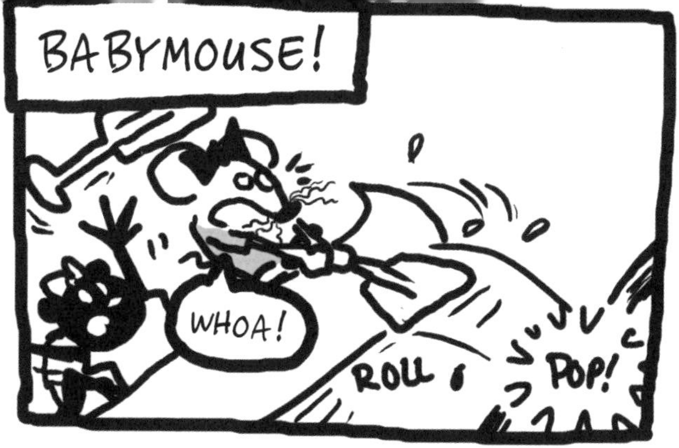
BABYMOUSE!
WHOA!
ROLL
POP!
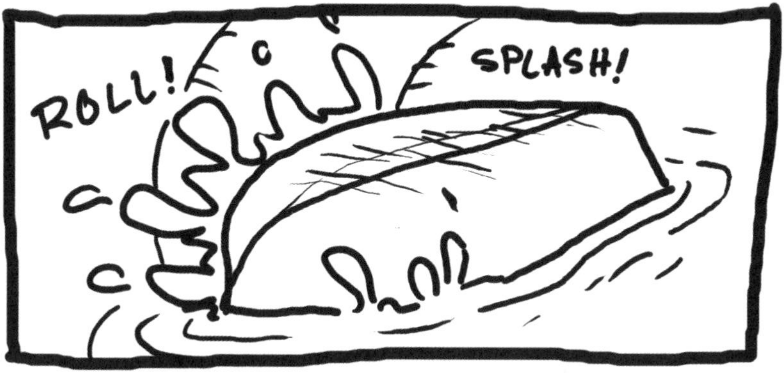
ROLL!
SPLASH!
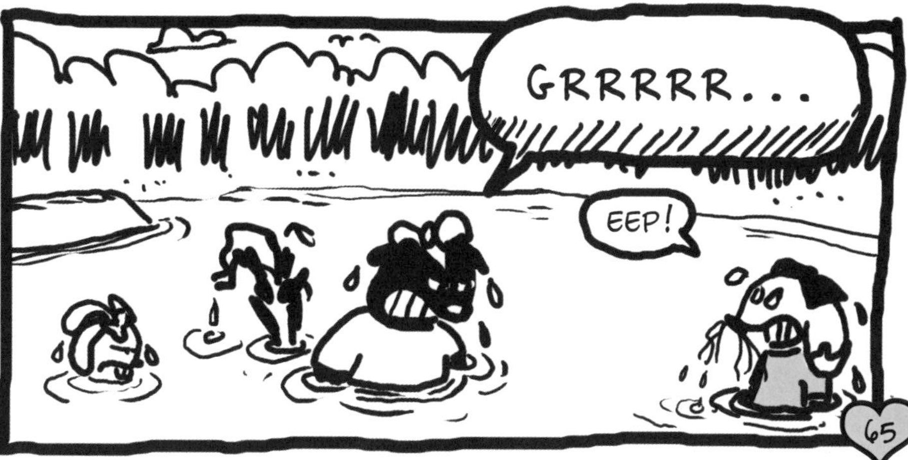
GRRRRR...
EEP!

67

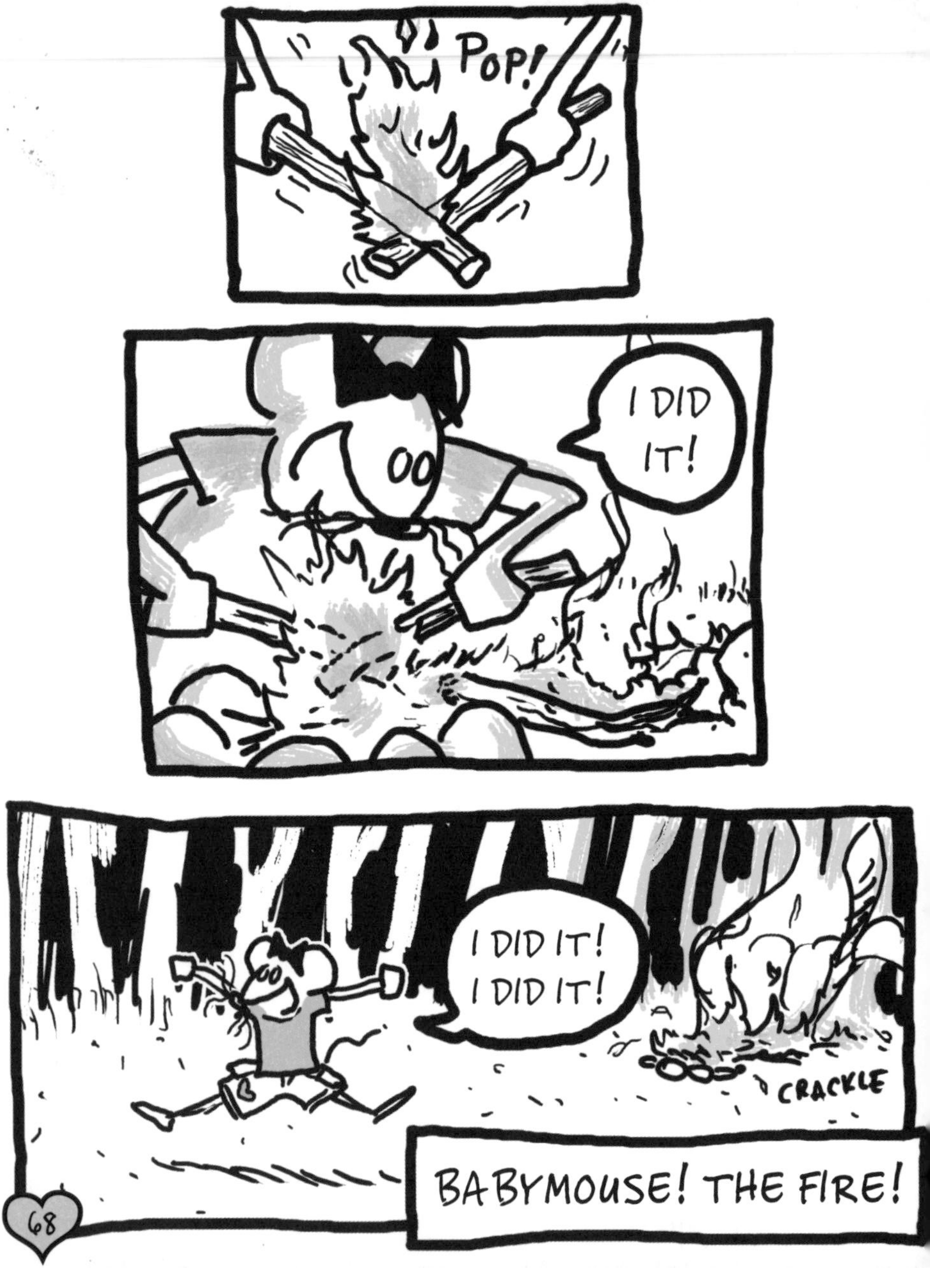
POP!
I DID IT!
I DID IT! I DID IT!
CRACKLE
BABYMOUSE! THE FIRE!

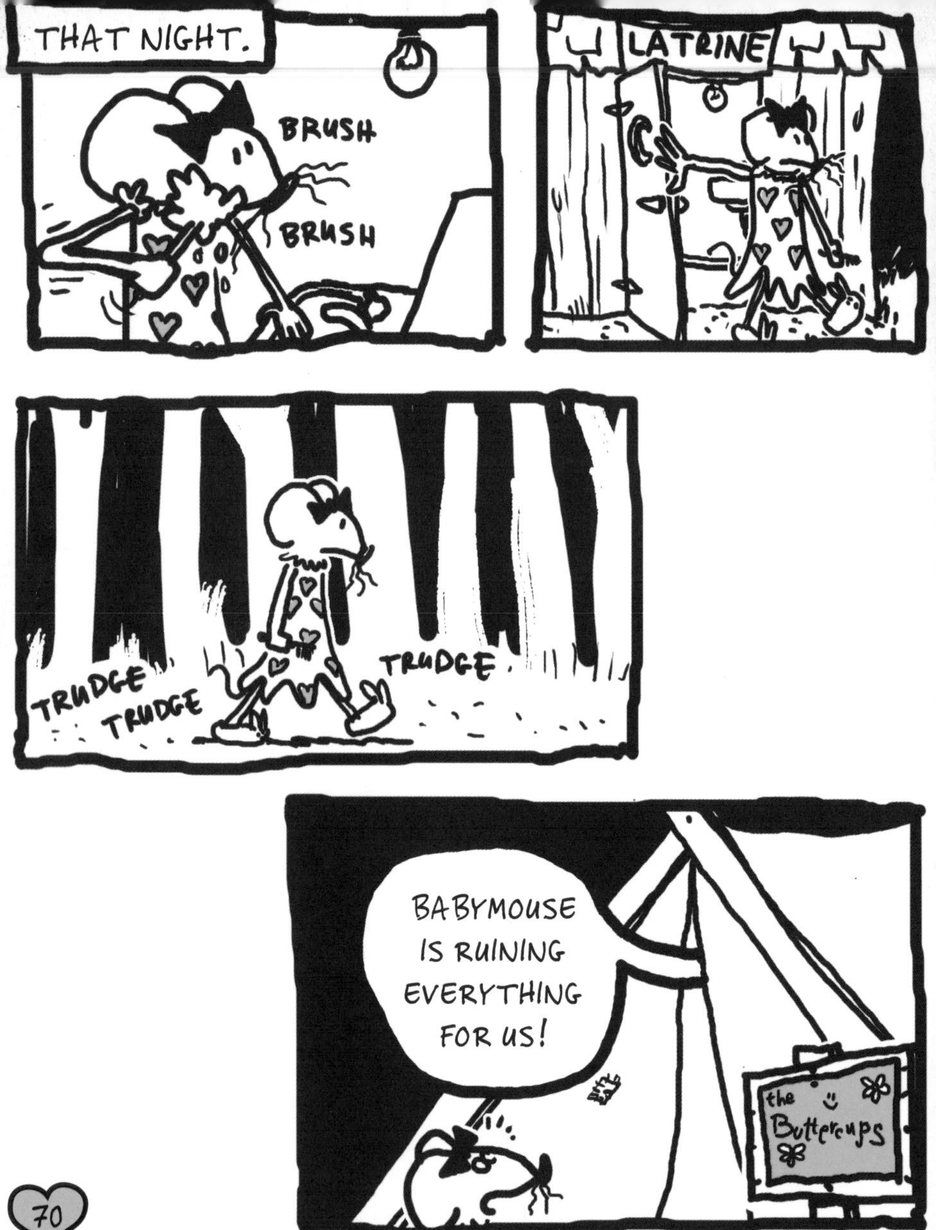
THAT NIGHT.
BRUSH
BRUSH
LATRINE
TRUDGE
TRUDGE
TRUDGE
BABYMOUSE IS RUINING EVERYTHING FOR US!
the Buttercups

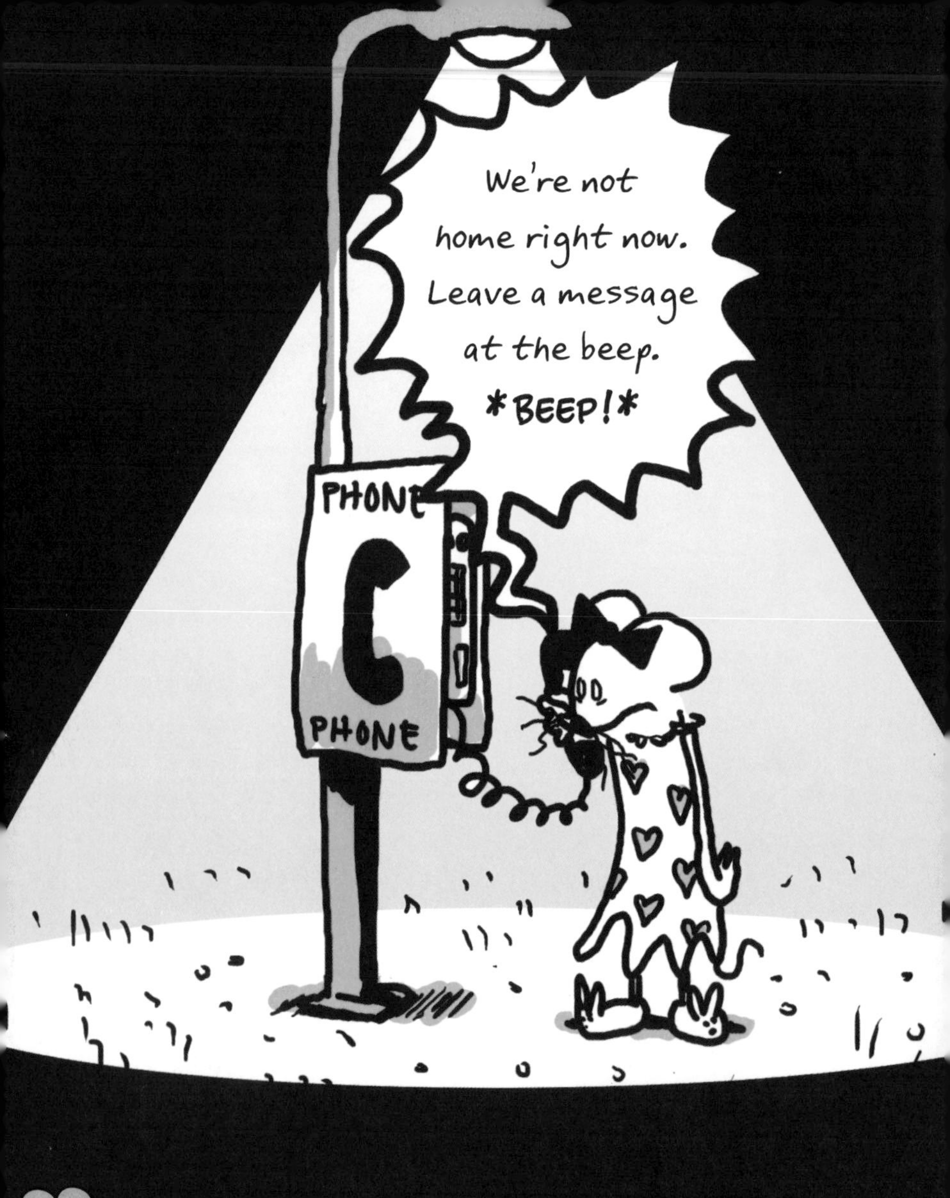

We're not home right now. Leave a message at the beep.
BEEP!
PHONE
PHONE

73

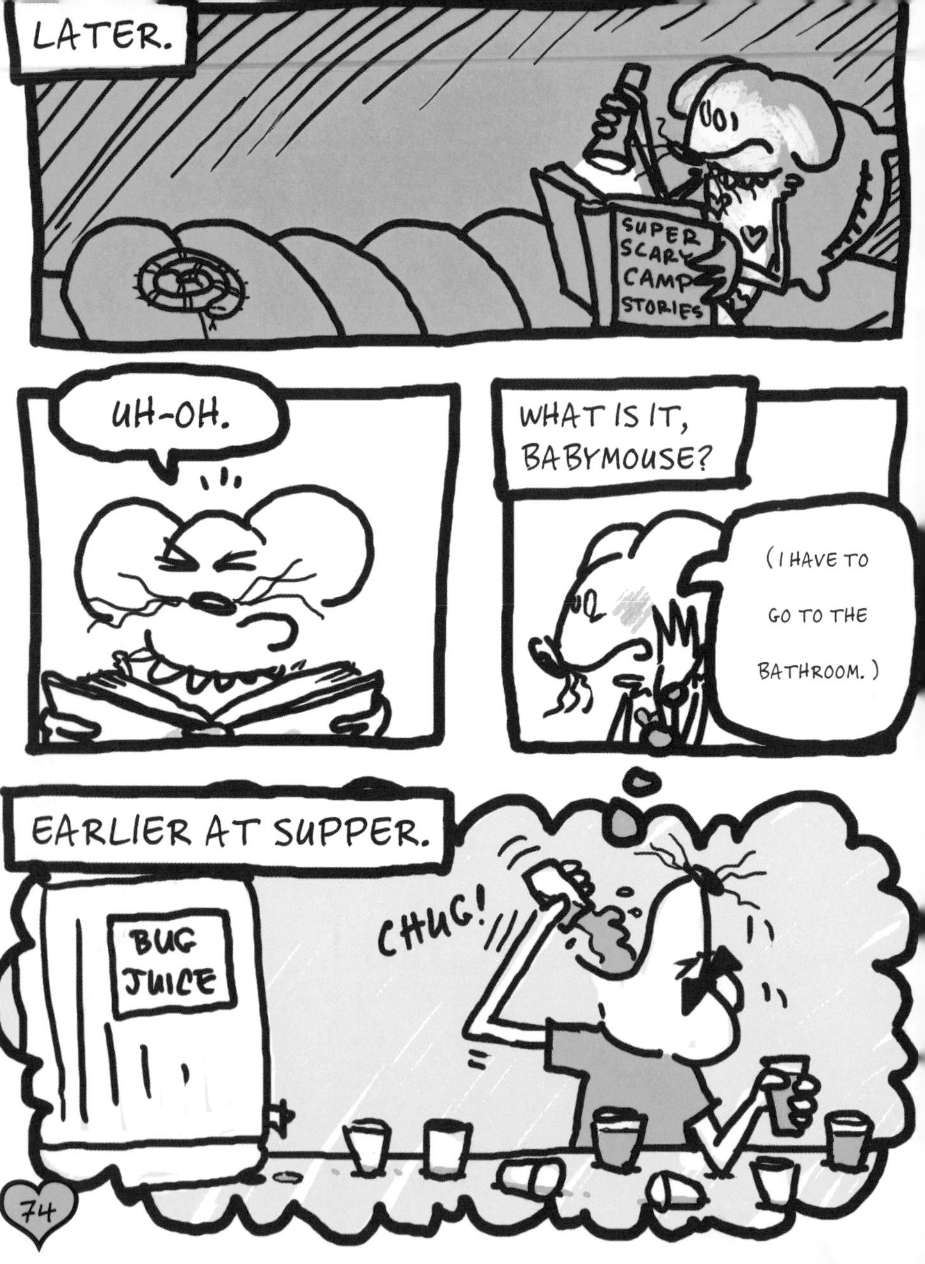
LATER.
SUPER SCARY CAMP STORIES
UH-OH.
WHAT IS IT, BABYMOUSE?
(I HAVE TO GO TO THE BATHROOM.)
EARLIER AT SUPPER.
BUG JUICE
CHUG!

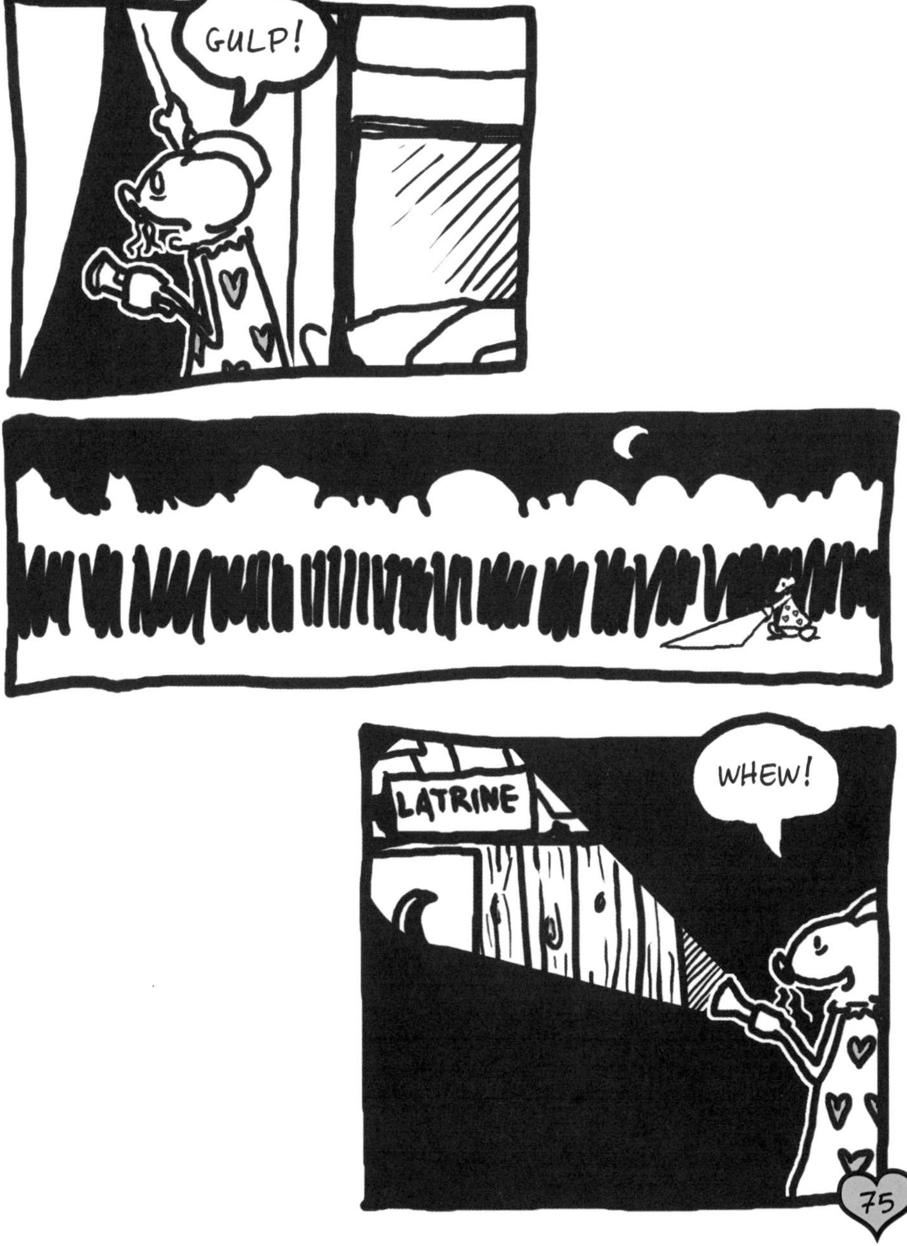
GULP!
LATRINE
WHEW!

PARKING
LOT

NORTH WOODS

CROOKED
TREE

LATRINE

START HERE

BIG
ROCK

WATERFALL

BONFIRE CIRCLE

PAY PHONE

MESS HALL

CABIN 7

DOCK

LAKE

BEACH

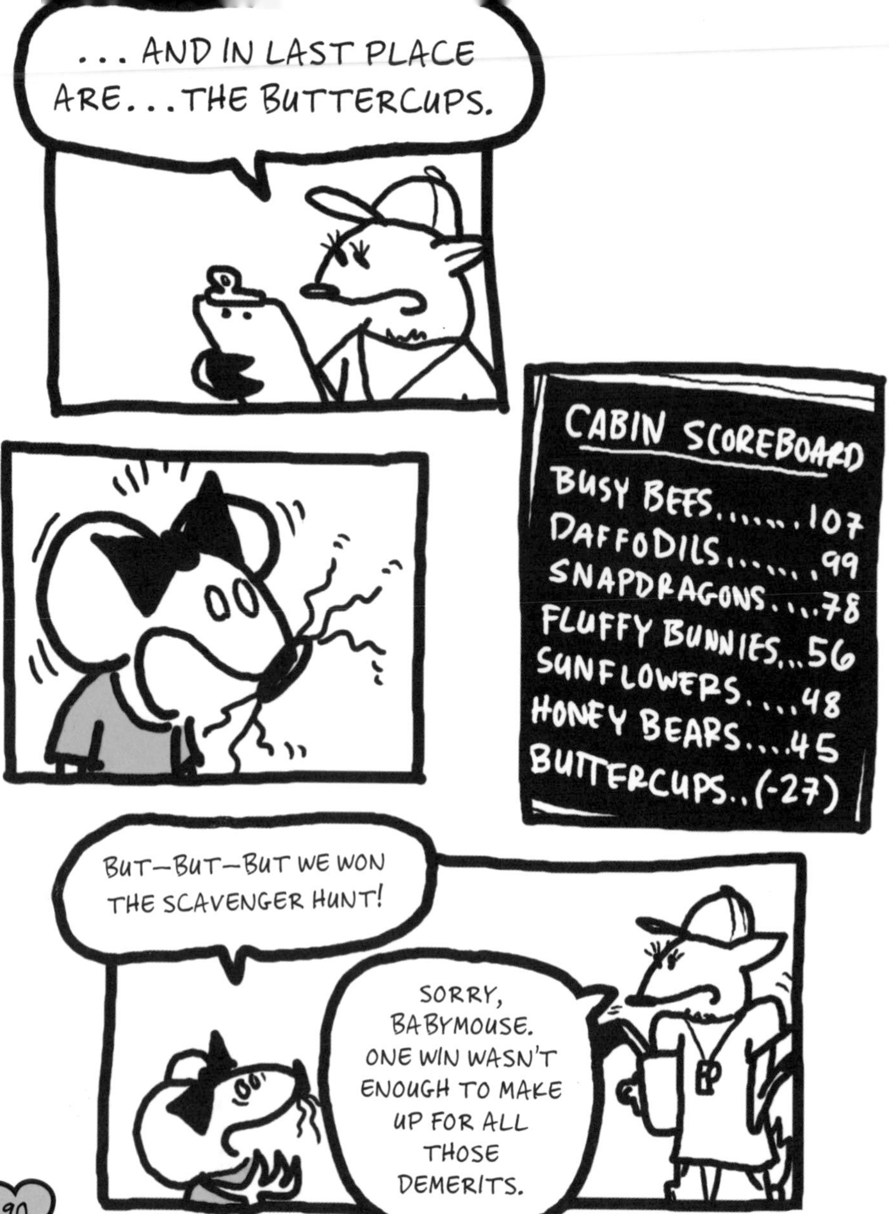

... AND IN LAST PLACE ARE... THE BUTTERCUPS.
CABIN SCOREBOARD
BUSY BEES.......107
DAFFODILS.......99
SNAPDRAGONS.....78
FLUFFY BUNNIES...56
SUNFLOWERS.....48
HONEY BEARS....45
BUTTERCUPS..(-27)
BUT—BUT—BUT WE WON THE SCAVENGER HUNT!
SORRY, BABYMOUSE. ONE WIN WASN'T ENOUGH TO MAKE UP FOR ALL THOSE DEMERITS.

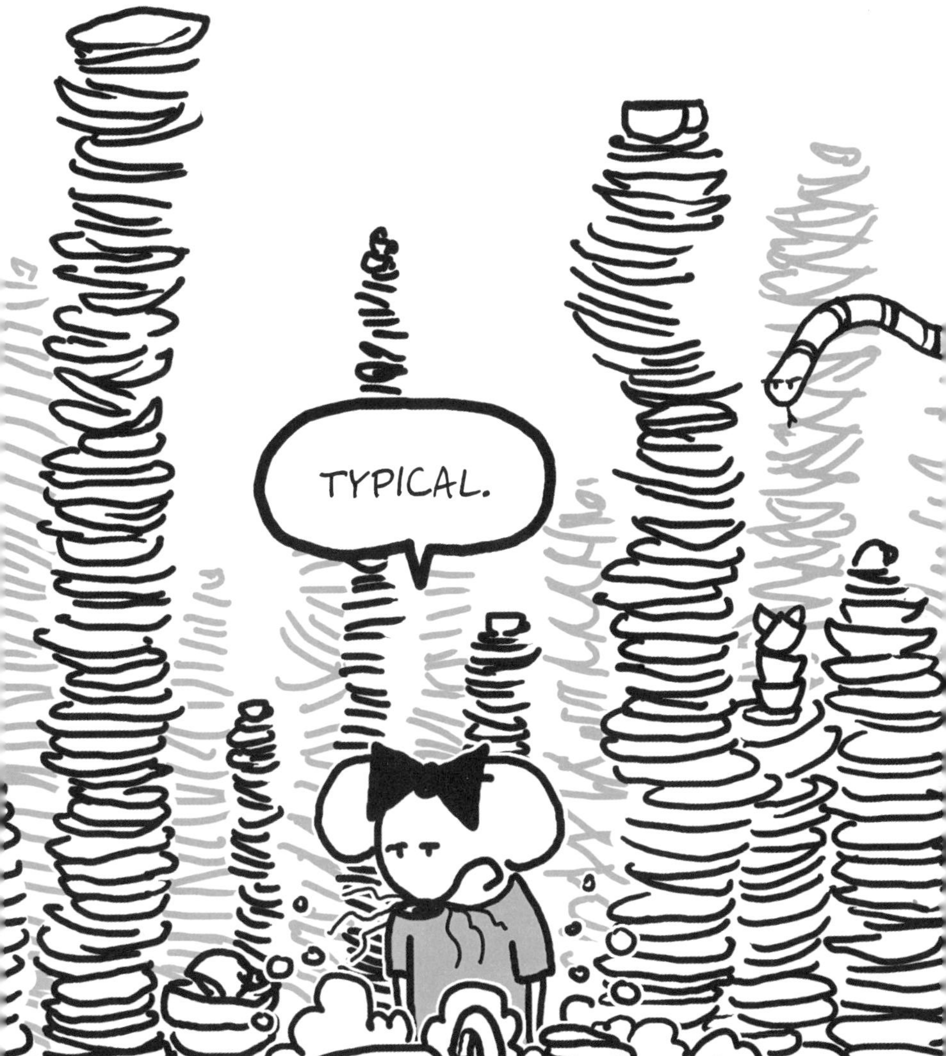
TYPICAL.

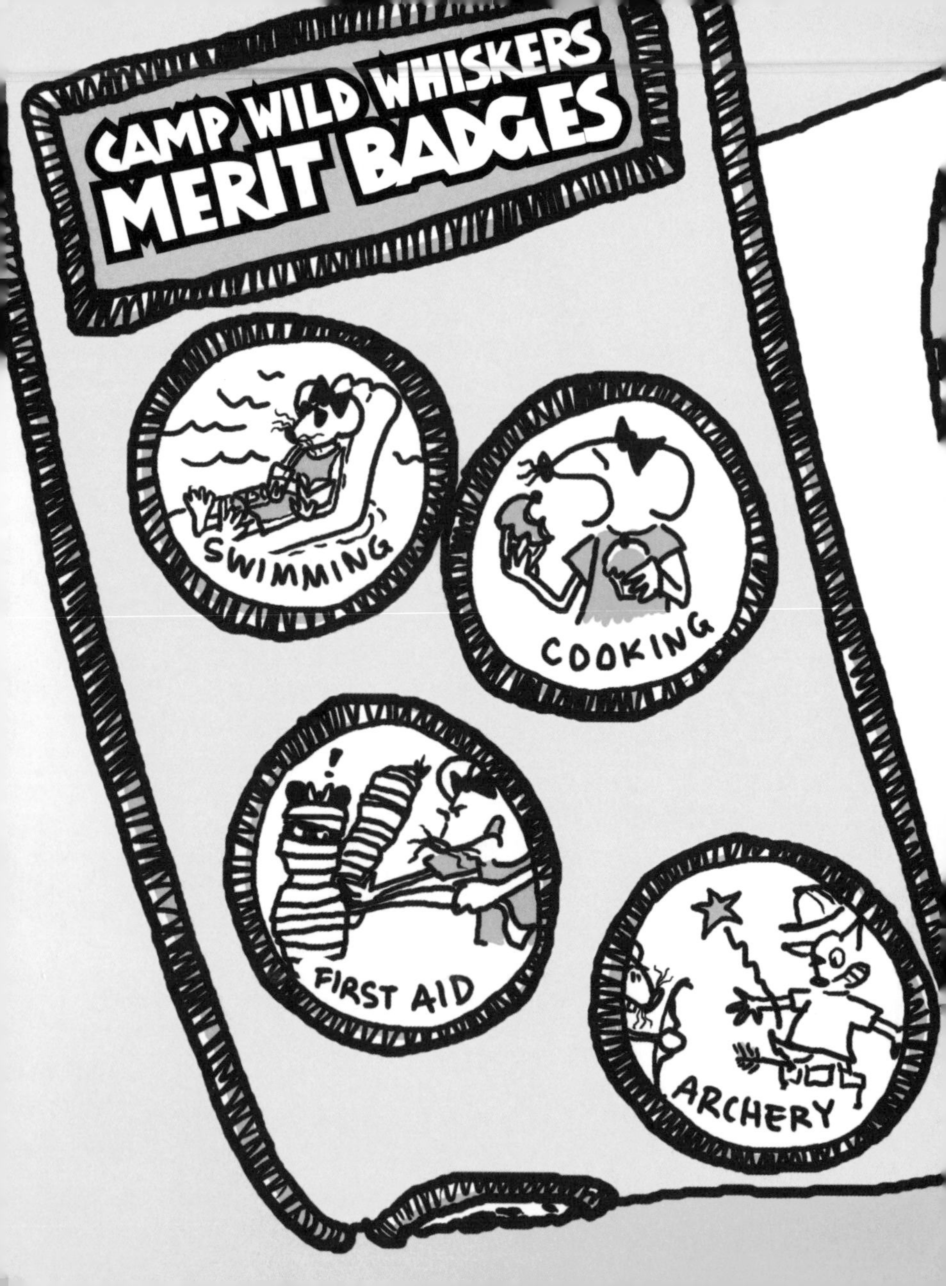
CAMP WILD WHISKERS
MERIT BADGES
SWIMMING
COOKING
FIRST AID
ARCHERY

BABYMOUSE BONUS!

• TIPS ON BEING A CAMPER •

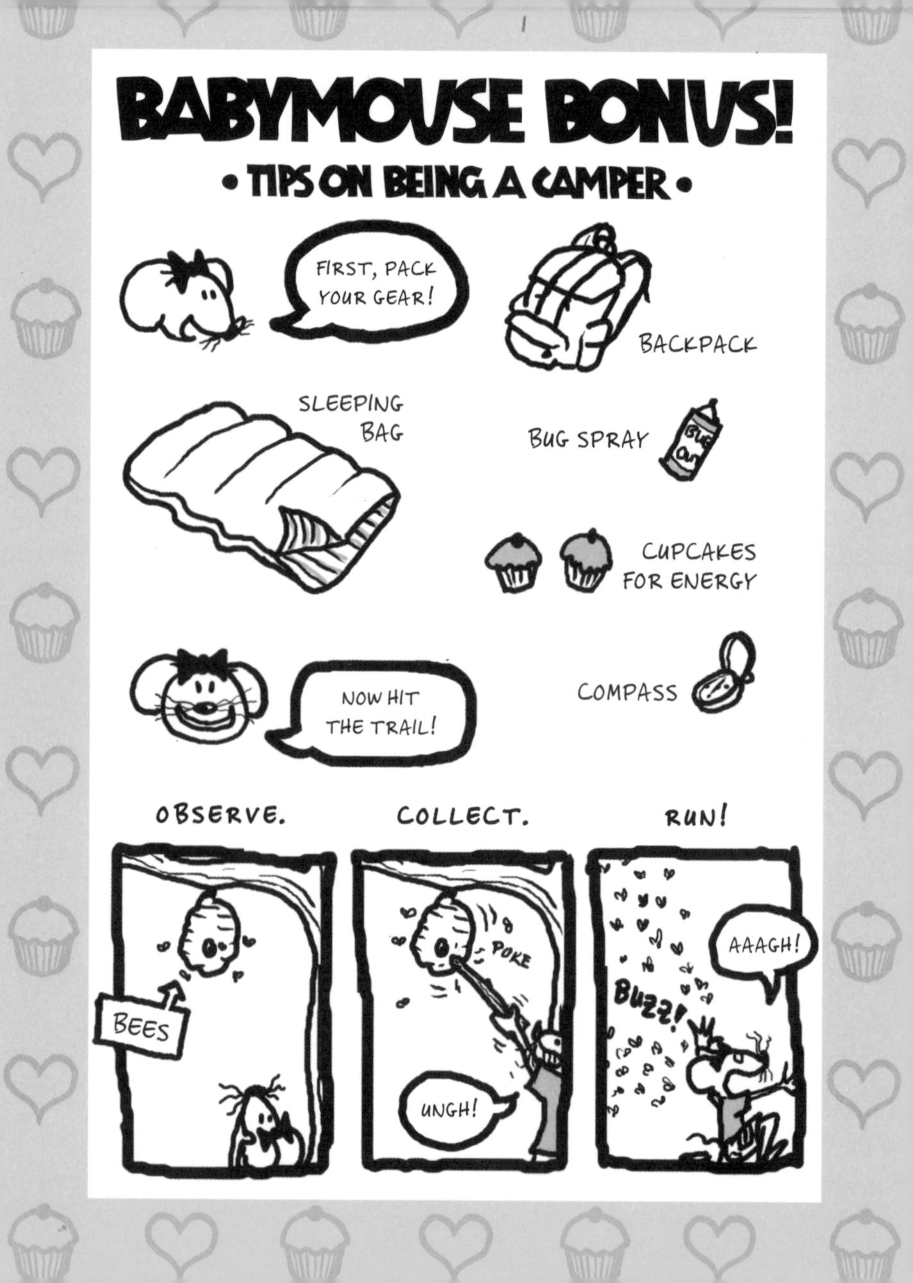
FIRST, PACK YOUR GEAR!
BACKPACK
SLEEPING BAG
BUG SPRAY
BUG OUT
CUPCAKES FOR ENERGY
NOW HIT THE TRAIL!
COMPASS
OBSERVE.
BEES
COLLECT.
POKE
UNGH!
RUN!
BUZZ!
AAAGH!